LONESOME REUNION

LONESOME REUNION

A LONESOME, PARTY OF SIX NOVEL

A. AINSWORTH

LONESOME, PARTY OF SIX SERIES

THE CARDS

"Hey, Dad, I'm back with the new lights for the tree. Here's your mail."

"His name is Bruce."

"Yeah, well, I'm not calling your tree by a name. You can forget that."

"Your loss. He's good company, Bruce is." Pops sorted through the stack without expectation. "Bill, bill, junk, junk, junk. Wait, what's this? I've already gotten the usual Christmas cards." His right index finger slid under the seal.

"What is it, Dad? Who's it from?" James Junior asked when he saw Pops wiping away a tear from his eye. Without explanation, Pops handed the card to his son. The cover read MERRY CHRISTMAS in gold script letters emblazoned above a manger scene. James Junior opened it and studied the handwritten words:

DEAR MR. JIMMY LEE,

I HOPE YOU ENJOY THE BEST CHRISTMAS OF YOUR LONG LIFE. MAY THE GOD WHO KNOWS YOUR NAME BLESS YOU DURING THIS SEASON AND THROUGHOUT THE NEW YEAR. I LOOK FORWARD TO MEETING YOU ON THE FOURTH THURSDAY OF NOVEMBER AT THE LOG CABIN.

LOVE,

LATICIA'S FRIEND

"Is THERE something you're not telling me?" asked Jane Fortenberry, the church's part-time secretary.

"I don't expect so," Pastor Hobbs answered. "Why?"

She held a large pink envelope aloft. The sender had sealed the flap with a row of red heart stickers. "You have a valentine."

"Don't move a muscle," he said. "If this is someone's idea of a joke, I'll need you to be a witness so something doesn't get started later." He peeled back the stickers and opened the envelope. "Oh my word," he muttered.

"What is it?"

"Do you remember last Thanksgiving when I told you somebody paid for a meal for those of us were eating alone at The Log Cabin?"

"Sure do. It's all you talked about until Christmas."

"Well, take a gander at this." He handed Jane the card, which she read aloud.

DEAR PASTOR HOBBS,

MAY THE LOVE YOU GIVE TO OTHERS COME BACK TO YOU MANY TIMES TODAY. I'M PRAYING YOU EXPERIENCE THE LOVE OF GOD THIS VALENTINE'S DAY AND THAT HE ALLOWS YOU TO FEEL JANIE RUTH'S LOVE TODAY, TOO. I LOOK FORWARD TO MEETING YOU ON THE FOURTH THURSDAY OF NOVEMBER AT THE LOG CABIN.

LOVE,

LATICIA'S FRIEND

"HERE'S THE IMPORTANT STUFF," Sherrill said, handing Easton his mail from the last few days. "How was the conference?"

"The usual—a bunch of salesmen cooped up together for three days selling each other on themselves and trying to appear busier than the next guy."

"Sounds like someone I know... or used to know."

"Not the same this year, for sure."

"Get away to check out the sights?"

"As a matter of fact, I did. After I did my presentation on Wednesday morning, I took the rest of the afternoon off and caught a ball game."

"You... went... to a *base*ball game? How was that?"

"Terrific. I went by myself, sat in the cheap seats. Ate a hot dog. Bought some peanuts and cracker jacks."

"Let me guess—you didn't care if you ever got back?"

He grinned, surprised she recognized the song. "I stood and sang along during the seventh inning stretch. Didn't consider lost opportunities, just chatted with the locals and had a tremendous time. Here, I bought you a T-shirt from the stadium store. You wear T-shirts sometimes, don't you?"

"Of course. And thanks, it's cute. Hey, something else came in the mail for you. It looks like a personal card, so I didn't want to open it. Resembles a woman's writing—something you need to tell me?"

"Nope. But it's not Mom's or Grace's handwriting. I have no idea who else would send me a card. You're welcome to spy on me as I open it, though."

"I believe I will," Sherrill said, always interested in

seeing how Easton responded in situations he didn't control.

He opened the envelope with caution, trying desperately to figure out its sender before he revealed it to Sherrill. It relieved him to pull out a card that wished him a happy Easter. "Must be from the church."

"Open it."

"Hold your horses." He opened the card and stopped when he read the brief note to himself:

HI, EASTON,

I HOPE YOU ENJOY A WONDERFUL EASTER WEEKEND CELEBRATING OUR RISEN SAVIOR. PLEASE TAKE TIME FOR YOUR FAMILY AND THE IMPORTANT PEOPLE IN YOUR LIFE. I LOOK FORWARD TO MEETING YOU ON THE FOURTH THURSDAY OF NOVEMBER AT THE LOG CABIN.

LOVE,
LATICIA'S FRIEND

"Sounds as though you have a secret admirer," Sherrill teased.

"No, remember last Thanksgiving when I was in Harriston?"

"How could I forget? The night someone ate my old boss?"

"Stop with the *boss* stuff. You know I hate that term."

Sherrill's eyes gleamed. "Do you hate it that much, boss?"

"Stop it," he said, shaking his head. "Anyway, I guess this solves one mystery of the night—whether our benefactor was a man or a woman. Laticia said she would pass along our thanks that night, so I figured it was a woman, someone she already knew. Until then, we guessed man because Pops said *he* bought our meal. Looks like I was right."

"HEY, HON?"

"Yes, dear."

"You got a card in the mail today. Personal, too." Irv handed the card to Carol, who perused the envelope.

"That's not Beth's or Kate's writing. Hmm, must be from Rebecca or Aliyah. That's sweet of them."

"Why would they send you a card? They'll be here with the boys for Mother's Day tomorrow."

Carol studied for a moment and created her own narrative before opening the card. "Perhaps one of them is just going the extra mile for their extra mother this year."

"One way to find out."

"Okay, here goes." She tore into the card, eager to see which daughter-in-law sent it. "It is a Mother's Day card, all right." Carol's fingertips flew to cover her mouth while she read the perfect cursive inscription to herself.

"Rebecca or Aliyah?"

"Neither."

"Who, then? Do you have another kid I don't know about? Read it."

HI, CAROL,

YOU'VE NEVER MET ME, BUT YOU ARE ONE MOTHER I ADMIRE VERY MUCH. YOUR STORY CONTINUES TO INSPIRE ME. HERE'S HOPING YOUR HUSBAND HAS FULLY RECOVERED AND IS DOING WELL AND THAT THIS MOTHER'S DAY IS THE BEST ONE YOU'VE EVER HAD WITH YOUR FOUR WONDERFUL CHILDREN. I LOOK FORWARD TO MEETING YOU ON THE FOURTH THURSDAY OF NOVEMBER AT THE LOG CABIN.

LOVE,

LATICIA'S FRIEND

CAROL SET the card on the kitchen counter and folded her arms. "It's from my secret friend who bought my meal last Thanksgiving."

"Wonder how she got our address?"

"Shouldn't have been too hard for Laticia to find it and give it to her?"

"Laticia?"

"Our hostess who coordinated our gathering."

"Oh, yeah, I just forgot her name."

"This is so sweet of her. I suspect there is no Laticia's friend, but that she *is* that friend."

"You think?"

"I'm not sure. What I realize for sure is it was a

7

perfect group to spend two hours with during a lonely time for all of us."

"So you're saying my heart attack wasn't so inconvenient like you enjoy calling it?"

She snuggled next to Irv. "I wouldn't go that far, dear, but I'm looking forward to showing off my healthy husband to my new friends on Thanksgiving night."

———————

"HEY, MOM."

"Hey, kiddo. Whatcha got there?"

"The mail."

"Any checks for me?"

"Nope, bills. This one looks like a card."

"A card? Hmm, wonder from whom?"

"Well, it's not Christmas or your birthday or Valentine's Day." Lisa Gull cocked her head to the side. "Mom, is there a certain someone you've neglected to tell me about? Maybe the new guy down in 4A?"

"What, him? No. Just no."

"He was being extra friendly to you when he helped us bring the groceries in on Saturday."

"You caught that, too, huh? Well, no danger of his courtesy turning into anything else. I don't entertain the slightest interest in him. My focus is on your brother's flight coming in at 2:36 this afternoon—or should I say fourteen thirty-six hours? I can't wait to see him!"

"Me either. As far as Mr. 4A, it appears he might *entertain the slightest interest* in you. Check it out, red envelope and everything," Lisa said, handing it to her mom.

Paula turned the envelope over in her hands, searching for clues. She opened her mouth to remark that the handwriting didn't resemble a man's when a knock at the door interrupted her thoughts. She asked Lisa to answer the door. Thoughts of cards and the guy in 4A disappeared when she caught sight of her son standing in the doorway.

"David!" she screamed, dropping the card and racing to throw her arms around his neck. After one long hug and then another, she said, "I thought you were coming on the 2:36 flight."

"Couldn't wait to see you. I grabbed a seat on an earlier flight. If you had anything planned for my arrival later, I'm sorry, but I figured you wouldn't turn me away if I showed up early."

"We did and we won't."

"Well, I'll tell you what—why don't we get caught up and then I'll disappear and you can bring me home to whatever you have planned for later. I'll act surprised, I promise."

"Oh, I don't care about that. Sit down and tell us everything. Do you want anything to eat?"

"Yes, I'm starving. I want to hear the play by play of Lisa's engagement and everything else I've missed while I've been away."

"Mom is entertaining the thought of a new boyfriend," Lisa teased, throwing a quick wink in David's direction.

"Stop it," Paula retorted, but her kids had allied against her.

"Tell, tell," David said. "Can't leave you alone for three years without your getting yourself hitched."

"Nobody is getting hitched."

"Speak for yourself. I am!" Lisa said. She slid over beside David on the couch and showed him her ring.

"Nice," he said, giving it a once over. "So you're saying Mom might get one of these soon? Who's the lucky guy?"

"The courteous gentleman in 4A. His name is Rodney. He helped us bring in the groceries on Saturday, and he sent Mom a card she's scared to open."

Paula blushed. "I have no interest in Creepy Rodney or anybody else, thank you very much. But I have to admit I am interested in who would send me a card. Must be somebody who realized David was coming home today. Now where did I put that card?" She looked on the tables before spotting it on the floor. "Here, David, I'll prove to you that the mystery lover in 4A is nothing but a figment of your sister's overactive imagination."

"Maybe it's a proposal," Lisa teased. "Maybe he wrote you a note that says 'Will you marry me? Check yes, no, or maybe.'"

"You need to hush, kiddo. I've had about enough of your kidding."

Stooping over to pick up the card, Paula whispered a quick prayer that opening it in front of her kids would not embarrass her. The seal gave way, and she pulled out a card with *Happy Independence Day* emblazoned over fireworks exploding in the night. Relieved, she opened it.

HELLO, PAULA.

I HOPE THIS CARD FINDS YOU DOING WELL AND EAGER FOR THE SAFE RETURN OF YOUR SON. I CAN ONLY IMAGINE HOW PROUD OF HIM YOU MUST BE. PLEASE DON'T TAKE THIS AS CREEPY, BUT AFTER HEARING YOUR STORY, I RESPECT SO MUCH THE JOB YOU HAVE DONE AS A MOM. OTHER SINGLE MOMS COULD LEARN FROM YOU. I LOOK FORWARD TO MEETING YOU ON THE FOURTH THURSDAY OF NOVEMBER AT THE LOG CABIN.

LOVE,
LATICIA'S FRIEND

"Well," Lisa said, "spill the tea. Was it from him?"

"No, from a dear friend I have yet to meet."

Tara slid in next to Pops in her usual seat at church, holding a card in front of him. "I got one, too."

"From our benefactor?" Pops asked. He recognized the writing as that of their mystery friend. While visiting with Irv and Carol one day in early summer, he discovered she had received a Mother's Day card. When Easton had taken his family to the beach earlier in June, he had called ahead and asked to meet Pops for lunch. He had received a card, too. Tara had been hoping for one, but couldn't decide which holiday made sense for her.

"Yes, open it!" she whispered loud enough for everyone sitting near them to hear.

Pops fumbled to open the envelope. He pulled out a *Happy 1st Birthday* card. "I don't understand."

"Open it, open it!"

Pops opened the card, read it, and nodded. "Makes perfect sense. Congratulations."

"Thank you very much."

Pops smiled and read the card again.

DEAR TARA,

I HAVEN'T MET YOU PERSONALLY, BUT, EVEN SO, I'M INCREDIBLY PROUD OF YOU. TWELVE MONTHS SOBER!!! YOU POSSESS SO MUCH POTEN-TIAL AND HAVE ALREADY OVERCOME MORE ADVERSITY THAN MOST PEOPLE WILL FACE IN A LIFETIME. THAT'S A LOT OF MOMENTUM YOU ARE BUILDING. I PRAY FOR YOU EVERY DAY, AND I CAN'T WAIT TO SEE HOW GOD WILL USE YOU TO BLESS OTHERS. I LOOK FORWARD TO MEETING YOU ON THE FOURTH THURSDAY OF NOVEMBER AT THE LOG CABIN.

LOVE,

LATICIA'S FRIEND

LATICIA OPENED a text message from Austen. *I sent the last card today. I hope they don't think I'm creeping on them.*

THEY DON'T. *Pops was in here last week, and he has talked to three of the others about their cards, and, of course, he got his for Christmas. The ones he talked to said they considered them jim-dandy. His word.*

YOU BELIEVE *they will all come?*

POPS *and the ones he talked to are coming. I'm not sure about Pastor Hobbs and Army Mom, but I would think they would come if they haven't forgotten.*

SHOULD *I reach out to them again or leave it alone?*

LAST YEAR WAS SO MEANINGFUL — YOU *don't need to worry. Plus, you sending those cards is bound to make them a little more than curious.*

OKAY, *I will start buying the decorations. Less than a month away. I am so excited!*

AUSTEN

2

"**K**nock, knock. Am I early?"

"Maybe a little, but come on in, we ready for ya." Laticia fast walked across the room to greet Easton Sterling, who set down a large bag just in time to meet her embrace. "Come on in, Mr. Important. I want to introduce you to somebody." Pulling him by his sleeve, Laticia brought him face to face with Austen. "Easton Sterling, this is my friend Austen Thomason."

His disarming smile captured Austen's attention, but she tried her best not to show it. She extended her hand with a pleasant, "Nice to meet you."

Easton wrapped both of his hands around hers and met her eyes with his. "I owe you a great deal. This time last year, I didn't realize it, but my life was about to run off the rails. Because of your generosity, I stayed and listened to the stories of everybody else at that table. When Pastor Hobbs told his wife's story and the impact she made on so many people, I realized I needed to make a change. I gave my life to Jesus, and He restored me to God and to my family. I cannot adequately express how grateful I am for what you did last year, but thank you."

Austen choked out, "You're welcome."

"This has been the best year of my life," he continued. "The Lord has taught me how to relax and how to use what He has given me to honor Him. The thing is, I haven't seen a noticeable difference in sales. My clients seem to appreciate the new me better than the old one. At least they haven't gotten upset with me when I can't get back with them right away sometimes like I did before I... you know, changed." He stopped. "Listen at me rambling on. I showed up early, hoping you were already here. I want to hear your story."

Austen told him about her job and her family and the circumstances that brought her to The Log Cabin the previous year. She surprised herself by the ease with which she talked to this handsome near stranger. He asked about her faith, and she related her story of giving her life to Christ at twelve and how a mission trip to Haiti had solidified her faith.

"Haiti, huh? I've got someone you need to meet. My executive coordinator works with an organization that does tremendous work there. Where did you go?"

"Jacmel."

"She has been to Thorman and Galette Chambon." And there it was: *she.*

Laticia asked what Austen dared not. "Just you, Mr. Important?"

"Come on, can't we move on to *Easton* this year?"

"Yeah, I'm just messing with you."

"I gotcha. No, I brought a guest. I recall we said that was okay. She's back at the hotel, but she'll be here by six."

Laticia noticed a quick flash of disappointment on Austen's countenance.

"Anybody else here yet?"

"Yes, Mr. Sterling, somebody else is here." The threesome turned to see Pastor Hobbs entering the door. Easton covered the twenty feet between them in no time to greet his friend. "Pastor, let me introduce you to the woman who started this. Pastor Calvin Hobbs, meet Austen Thomason." He shared several details Austen had shared with him. *No wonder he's such a fantastic salesman. He doesn't forget a thing.*

"Austen, such an honor to meet you at last. Last year's Thanksgiving was such a blessing to us. And that Valentine's card you sent me was so right on time—I can't tell you just how much that meant to me." After hugging Laticia, he said, "Hey, last year when we planned tonight, we said that it was okay to bring guests. I hope that's still okay."

Laticia waved her arm toward the tables. "We set up for thirty, and if we need more tables and chairs, I can make that happen in mere minutes."

Pastor Hobbs held up his right index finger. "I'll be right back." He returned to the room with a well-dressed lady around his age. "I would like to introduce you folks to my friend Vicki Stapleford."

Laticia, Easton, and Austen introduced themselves, but they could not hide their curiosity.

"I told Vicki about last year's meeting, and I thought it would encourage her to be a part of our group this year. I'll let her tell you her story."

Vicki took a deep breath. "I'll give you the play-by-play after everybody gets here, but my husband Roger was diagnosed with cancer in February, and he was gone not long after that. I went through the motions for a while, saying what I should say and doing what I thought I should do. Inside, though, such a sizable piece of me was missing. It was a double gut punch, losing my best friend and my husband within a year of each other. Calvin is the only person who could possibly understand. He suggested coming here tonight. He said I could talk if I wanted to talk and just listen if I didn't want to talk. I am determined to tell my story. Or let Calvin tell it. It involves him, too."

Just then, Pops walked through the door with James Junior. He looked spry in his dark blue jeans, plaid shirt, and loafers. He called out, "Hello, my friends!"

"Pops!" Easton called back. "And James Junior, how are you, buddy?"

James Junior stuck out his hand and greeted Easton, with whom he had joined his father to fish when Easton had visited. "Hey, Easton, good to see you."

"Come on over here, both of you. I want you to meet somebody special." He led them across the room to where Laticia and Austen were talking to Vicki. "Excuse me, ladies. I wanted to introduce my friends here to Austen. Austen, this is my friend Jimmy Lee Yates and his son, James. Nobody calls him James, though; we call him James Junior. Guys, meet Austen Thomason, our benefactor from last year."

Pops asked, "Young lady, would you mind if an old man gives you a hug?"

"No sir, it would be an honor."

"You did a fine thing here last year, Ms. Austen. I don't know what led you to do it, but it did a lot of good for all of us to get together and share our lives with one another. In my ninety-three years, I've never experienced anything like it."

"I'm glad it blessed you," Austen said. "You remember Pastor Hobbs, don't you?"

"Of course I do. We've talked since then. Good to see you again, Calvin."

"Nice to see you, too, Mr. Jimmy Lee. Here, I want you to meet my friend, Vicki."

"Good to know you, Vicki. Calvin told me about your husband. I'm sorry for your loss."

"Thank you, sir."

"This is my son, James Junior."

As James Junior and Vicki exchanged greetings, Paula Gull arrived with her son, daughter, and future son-in-law in tow. The introductions started again, with Easton recalling every name as he assumed the role of connecting everyone. Paula hugged Austen and thanked her for the Fourth of July card. They laughed when Paula informed her how it sparked an inquiry into her love life from Lisa and David.

When Tara Cates arrived, Easton stepped forward to introduce the two young ladies. "Tara... Austen. Austen... Tara."

Austen and Tara struck up a conversation as if they were old friends. After a few minutes of pleasantries, Tara asked, "How could you be sure I had made it through twelve months sober? I appreciate the card, but it was risky to send it."

"Not as much as you might imagine. I talked to Laticia, who visited with Pops every few weeks, and he saw you in church every week. I hope that doesn't sound like I was creeping on you. But I have been pulling so hard for you and praying for you ever since Laticia told me your story last Thanksgiving."

"Thank you very much. I wouldn't be standing here thirteen months clean without what you did last year, so, yeah, I'll forgive any creepiness."

WHEN THE TIME moved past six o'clock, Laticia ushered those gathered to the round tables, each set up to seat six. Pops and James Junior sat with Pastor Hobbs and Vicki Stapleford. Paula sat with Lisa, David, and Jake at another. Tara, Austen, and Laticia seated themselves at the table at the front of the room. After everyone else had taken their seats, Easton ventured toward the girls' table and asked to join them.

"I might be outnumbered, but it seems I don't fit as well at any of the other tables."

"You sit yourself on down," Laticia ordered. "Tell me how your year has been. Pops told me y'all ate here when you were down here during the year. I hate I wasn't working when you came."

"Yeah, me, too. We were hoping to visit with you. Well, ask away about my year."

Laticia dove right in. "You make things right with your family? That's a blessing, you understand, to have a family."

Easton remembered Pops' telling him Laticia's sad story of losing her family over the years. "I did, I did. We cooked out at my brother's house that Sunday night, and I made things right with him and my sister. I took off early on Monday afternoon and drove over to visit my mom, too. I drop by at least twice a week now, and I get her out and drive her around to some of her old familiar places on the weekend. She likes that, and her health seems to be improving. I'm afraid her loneliness did as much damage as the stroke."

"You went all in, didn't you?"

"You know my story. That's how I roll, for better or worse."

"Speaking of for better or worse..." Laticia started, but he held up his hand and stood.

"Excuse me, ladies, my date has arrived."

The three young ladies lifted their eyes to the doorway where a stunning brunette was waiting. She looked like a catalog model dressed down to the girl-next-door look. Easton met her with a friendly kiss on the cheek and held her hand as he led her back to the table.

"Austen, Tara, and Laticia, I'd like you to meet my lovely date for the evening..."

Laticia stood first and held out her hand. "I'm Laticia. Nice to meet you, Sherrill."

While the brown-eyed beauty stood with a confused look on her face, Easton cackled. "Wait, you thought… no, this is my sister, Grace Sterling Holliman."

Austen recovered first. "Sure, I notice the resemblance." *Good looks sure run in your family, Mr. Sterling.*

Easton took his sister from table to table, calling Grace's name first to the others to avoid the same confusion. Laticia excused herself to take drink orders but not before leaning over to whisper in Austen's ear, "Mm hm, girl, I see that look in your eye."

"Stop it. I don't guess Ms. Carol is going to make it?"

"It is getting on toward quarter after. I figured she would come. Here, let me ask Pops. He might have heard from her." Laticia walked toward the door, stopping to inquire about Carol and flashing a thumbs up toward Austen. In less than a minute, she returned with pad and paper in hand. She clapped her hands to get everyone's attention.

3

"We're about ready to get started, folks, but I wanted to take care of a few things before I take y'all's orders. How about a big round of applause for the young lady who made all of this possible? Her generosity allowed a few lonely people to have some community here at The Log Cabin last year."

The number of people applauding Austen grew louder when Irv and Carol Turner entered, complete with four children, two daughters-in-law, and their daughters' dates. They settled into the chairs at the two remaining tables when the applause subsided. Carol mouthed, "Sorry we're late."

Laticia continued, "I'm gonna let Austen tell her story in a minute, but I wanted to give y'all some news first. Some of y'all know this already, but I've taken a new position at the Log Cabin corporate office in Charlotte. I couldn't imagine any better way to spend my last day at this job than to serve you folks and visit with you one more time." Turning to her right, she said, "All right, Austen. Have I bought you enough time?"

"Tell you what," Austen answered. "Give me a few minutes to meet Carol's family, and I'll say a few words. I didn't realize I was to give a speech tonight."

Laticia grinned. "You just talk, Austen. We ain't going anywhere. You've got a captive audience."

Austen spent a few minutes meeting Irv and Carol, Jeremiah and Rebecca, Isaiah and Aliyah, and Beth and Kate and their dates. She wished she could spend an entire evening with each member of Lonesome, Party of Six. Determined to squeeze the most from the next couple of hours, she strode to the front of the room. By then, Laticia had taken everyone's drink orders and was handing out sweet teas, waters, and cokes. Austen tapped a spoon against her glass of sweet tea to command everyone's attention.

"Hi, everybody, I understand I've met you already, but I'll start with hey, I'm Austen. I tell stories for a living through graphic design and copywriting for small businesses and non-profit organizations. I never considered when I woke up last Thanksgiving Day that I would find myself in a story of my own. Neither did you, but here we are.

"I woke up that day feeling out of sorts. My brother is a student at Mississippi State, and he stayed in Starkville for the Egg Bowl that day. That threw our normal family Thanksgiving at my grandmother's house back a day and left my immediate family scrambling for something to do. My parents and my little brother and I went to a movie that afternoon. The young boy in the movie was lonely, and I could relate, even though we had very little else in common." *Should I tell them about Mick? Nah, I'll let that slide.* "One of his class-mates did something kind for him, and it changed the entire direction of his life. The last line of the movie said something like, 'You never comprehend how the smallest intentional act of kindness might change some-body's everything.' That line stuck with me, and I was still pondering it when my family came here to eat.

"Laticia and I attended high school together. Even though we weren't close friends, she was always nice to me, and I was glad to see her friendly face when we walked in. She seemed unusually cheerful to be working on such a busy holiday, so I asked about that. She walked me into the dining room and started pointing out the people in there eating alone for Thanks-giving. A year ago, you were six random strangers for whom I empathized, even though I was eating with my family. Maybe you have felt alone in the middle of a crowd like me?" Austen noticed nods across the room. "I considered the people surrounding the little boy in the movie. Most of them sympathized for him, but they acted helpless to give him the encouragement he needed. Some feared how he might react, and others froze because they couldn't figure out what to say. His one friend did something by making him a valentine for their class party, the only card he received, but it made him smile that not everybody had forgotten him.

"You looked like normal people I might pass on the street every day without a second glance. But on Thanksgiving, you were conspicuous, and if you needed just one person to notice you, I wanted to be that person. Do you guys mind if I read something from the Bible to you?"

Everyone nodded their assent. Austen walked to her table to retrieve her phone. She opened her Bible app and read from Matthew 25:31-40:

"When the Son of Man comes in his glory, and all the angels with him, then he will sit on his glorious throne. Before him will be gathered all the nations, and he will separate people one from another as a shepherd separates the sheep from the goats. And he will place the sheep on his right, but the goats on the left. Then the King will say to those on his right, 'Come, you who are blessed by my Father, inherit the kingdom prepared for you from the foundation of the world. For I was hungry and you gave me food, I was thirsty and you gave me drink, I was a stranger and you welcomed me, I was in prison and you came to me." Then the righteous will answer him, saying, 'Lord, when did we see you hungry and feed you, or thirsty and give you drink? And when did we see you a stranger and welcome you, or naked and clothe you? And when did we see you sick or in prison and visit you?' And the King will answer them, "Truly, I say to you, as you did it to one of the least of these my brothers, you did it to me."

"Now, that passage doesn't expressly say, 'I was lonely and you gave me encouragement,' but it lines up with the rest of it. I don't deserve much credit for what happened last year. I just paid your bill with a little hope that it would put a smile on your face. Laticia—she's the one who showed me the need and made it happen and shared all your remarkable stories with me. She's the one we should thank for taking a lonely day for us and making it a day I'm sure none of us will ever forget. Why don't we give it up for Miss Corporate Hospitality?"

Everyone stood at Austen's invitation and clapped long and hard for Laticia until she made her way to Austen's side and wrapped her up in a bear hug. "Speech, speech!" started with Pops and soon filled the rest of the room.

"Aight, aight, gimme a minute to get some words together." Laticia needed a few seconds to catch her breath before she declared herself ready. "My mama died when I was in third grade. My daddy had already left us, and I honestly don't know whatever became of him. He moved off and never came back." At this, she captured Lisa and David Gull's attention. "I was determined to be somebody with or without my parents, even at that young age. My grandparents took me in, and they were some fine folks—did me right. I suppose they are why I have always been an old soul. They passed a few years back. I miss them every day.

"Mama and me were on government assistance, and my grandparents weren't much better off. I worked hard in school, though, and I got some scholarships and grants to help me get through community college. University is a lot more expensive, though. I've had to pay for my own place since my grandparents passed because it took everything I got from selling their house to pay for their funerals and a few bills they had. I determined I wasn't going to take on loans—grew up way too poor for that. It took me a while to get through, sitting out a semester here and there to save money and pay my bills." She winked at Pastor Hobbs, knowing his college journey was difficult, too. "I'm gonna walk across that stage and get my paper in two weeks, and I'll be in Charlotte before Christmas to get started with Log Cabin corporate."

Laticia started back to her table after the guests applauded. "Is that it?" Paula asked. "Sounded like you were just getting started good."

"Well, my boyfriend is going be moving to Charlotte, too. He just got a job out there. I don't want to put the cart ahead of the horse, but if we both like it out there, we're talking about getting married. We're gonna live separate out there for a while and make up our minds next summer."

"Wow, seems like everybody is moving to Charlotte. My favorite weatherman at Channel 7—that Robert Jones— is moving out there, too… wait…"

Laticia grinned.

"No way," Paula said. "He's a good catch."

"He's a good man, too. Loves Jesus, loves people."

"Well, you're quite the catch yourself. Best of luck."

"Thank you very much. Well, enough about me. Y'all want some dessert, right? This might be my last night, but pie don't serve itself." Everybody laughed and let her go. As she walked out, she turned back around and said, "Austen, girl, this is your party. Take over."

TARA

4

Austen looked the room over and asked, "Why don't we go in the same order as last year and each of you give an update on your life since last year. Some of us might not know each other well, but I hope you will feel comfortable enough to share how your life has changed since one year ago today. Okay, who's first?"

"I think that would be me," Pops said, rising to his feet.

"Actually," Tara interrupted, "I told you my story first in the shopping area out front, and then everybody else joined us. I'm not sure the rest of the original Lonesome, Party of Six have heard my full story."

"You're right," Pops said. He pointed toward the front of the room. "After you, then."

Tara walked to the front of the room and smiled to her new friends.

"Okay, here goes. The short version of my backstory

goes like this: I am a drunk who is now thirteen months sober, my longest stretch since middle school. I might as well have been kicked out of my parents' house when I got pregnant at fifteen. My aunt gave me a second chance, and my great-grandmother gave me a third. Both of them were watching my little boy—Zan is his name—when they died of heart attacks. I was out drunk both times, and the second time led to child services taking Zan away from me. My parents were gracious to take him in and give him a stable home and allow me to continue living in my great-grandmother's house while I got clean. They showed you can love your child without liking her. I understand that without consistent accountability, I'm liable to step back into that life I hate, but it still calls me sometimes."

Tara paused at the response of her no-holds-barred summary. "I'm sorry, y'all. I am so used to sharing my story with drunks and addicts who never bat an eye when I share it, but I can be myself here among you, too, right?" Everyone nodded, encouraging her to go on. Throwing her brown-haired ponytail over her right shoulder, she continued with a composure she hadn't possessed in their prior meeting.

"Well, last year, mine was a story of desperation. I noticed a liquor store right down the street on my way here to eat a lonely Thanksgiving meal. The longer I was here, the more that liquor store called me. I had an hour to kill before my sponsor made it home, and that hour might have killed me. Austen, if you hadn't paid for our meals last year, Mr. Jimmy Lee wouldn't have stopped me to talk, and I would have gone straight there to wipe out a month of hard work to stay sober. Today, I want to tell you guys about some trophies I've picked up in the last thirteen months.

"When most people think about Celebrate Recovery, they focus on the *recovery* part. That is mostly what we're about, but celebrating is a big part of keeping our momentum going. And, y'all, momentum is everything to an addict. Before I met all of you guys last year, I picked up a blue chip that meant I was surrendering my addiction to alcohol to Jesus. I'll be honest, though, I didn't stand up to walk forward and get my chip until several other people did. When I made it through thirty days—that was the Friday night before we all met—I received a red chip, which reminds us of the blood of Christ and His forgiveness. That one meant a little more to me, but I was about to throw away my progress when I had an hour to spare and a liquor store in sight.

"Instead, I stuck with it to pick up a green chip at sixty days sober and a white chip at ninety days. Every chip is a reminder of some aspect of Christ. The white chip reminds of the purity of Jesus and the purity we can have through His work on the cross. That's when I came to the end of myself and realized I was still trying to do this whole sobriety thing depending on my willpower and CR meetings and my sponsor.

"I had been attempting to follow a Savior I hoped would save me from alcohol. I wanted Him for what He could do for me. Deep down, though, I still believed no one would care more for my life than I could. My sponsor asked me, 'Tara, what happens when you are in control of your own life?' I had to admit I steered myself into the ditch time after time. When Aunt Suzanne gave me an opportunity to rebuild my life, I did fine until she started giving me some freedom. That's when I drove off a cliff, so to speak. When my granny did the same thing, I reached such a healthy place, but my old demons blindsided me. I didn't deny that an unaccountable hour and a liquor store down the street almost wrecked me again. My sponsor led me to Jesus that night, and my life changed forever. I'm letting Jesus lead the way now. Still, small round colored tokens are powerful motivators. I kept picking up coins every thirty days until I achieved this." Tara held up her phone and walked around until everyone had seen the photo of her beaming as she held her one-year coin.

"I have another coin I'm even more proud of, one that represents my completion of all twelve steps of the recovery process. I had such momentum by this time that ten of the steps were—I wouldn't say easy, but I was ready for them. Step eight was tough, though, making a list of all persons I harmed and being willing to make amends with them. Actually, step eight wasn't so bad because I did nothing except make the list, but step nine is actually making those amends when possible. I live every day with the inability to make amends to Aunt Suzanne and Granny, but my parents and my brother were another story—especially my mom and John David. I will have a deeper conversation with Zan when he's older, too." Tara's smile reflected the pain she still carried.

"I started with my dad as a dress rehearsal for the tougher conversations. I tried not to treat it that way, though, because his life turned upside down with all of my poor decisions, too. The week after I went to jail for a DUI—that's when child services took Zan from me— my dad started scheduling daddy-daughter dates with me every week, just the two of us. Mom didn't know about most of our dates. It appeared Dad was trying to reach out in his own way to rebuild my connection with the family and hoping Mom and John David would come around at some point. All that to say, I brought up my need to make amends with Dad easily enough since we met on the regular, anyway.

"I asked if Dad minded meeting for breakfast instead of lunch one Friday morning. He would be driving straight from his men's group, and I wanted to catch him in his best frame of mind for what I was going to tell him. I wasn't two minutes in before he cut me off and told me my offenses weren't against him, and he had long since forgiven me for how the fallout of my decisions affected him. He said the only amends he asked from me was to follow through on my intentions to pursue the tough conversations with Mom and my brother. He assured me if they didn't respond how we both hoped they would, we would believe I did every-thing possible, and the Lord could change their hearts in time.

"I waited a few weeks, going over and over what I said to my dad and trying to improve on my presenta-tion. Every time I replaced my dad's face with Mom's, the words rang hollow. One day at church, I told Mr. Jimmy Lee what I was trying to get up the nerve to do, and he said it was high time I heard my granny's story.

She sat in front of Pops at church for years and used to quote a passage from 1 Corinthians about comforting others with the same hope with which we have been comforted. When I mentioned that last year, he made the connection between me and Granny and asked if I had ever heard her story. I guess she got so caught up in helping me survive day by day that she forgot her own preaching—either that or she didn't want me to know her past. Anyway, when he told me her story, it gave me the courage to own mine with Mom."

5

The family gathering at the Reynolds' place was the first in a more than a year. The patriarch of the family, Bubba Reynolds, had shut down the last one and swore to his wife it was the last time he ever wanted to see those ungrateful, good-for-nothing kids of hers. They were his kids, too, but only when he could get some work out of them. For all the food he put on the table for them that day, they should have been more than willing to hop in the back of the old Chevy longbed truck and head over to the back side of the place to help him chop up that tree that had fallen over the creek. Mama had told them to stand up to him this time, to refuse to do whatever work he would inevitably guilt them into doing. She had their backs ... for whatever that was worth.

It's not that they were lazy or even unwilling. But their father's attitude of always having to be in charge had haunted them from their childhood. He ruled over his two hundred acres like an ancient lord ruling his fiefdom. Each of his five sons enlisted in the U.S. Army on the day he turned eighteen. The sons learned different trades, and each had carved out a decent living for himself. They had their struggles but became productive citizens. After the hell Bubba had put them through, that was a miracle in itself. Martha Reynolds prayed to God constantly for her boys and thanked Him every day that she and Bubba never produced a daughter.

When the boys refused to help Bubba cut up the wood, he threw an expletive-filled tantrum. They had seen it before and expected it that day. The collateral damage was their wives and children in the next room who feared Bubba might harm the five sons. Junior made the mistake of saying, "Mama told us we wouldn't have to work this time, that we could just come and enjoy being together as a family. Come on, Bubba, why does it always have to be this way?"

When his father struck him with a wicked right hand across his mouth, she stepped in to protect him as she always had. "Junior," she said with tears streaming down her face, "how dare you talk to your father that way. I think it's best you leave our house now. The rest of you can go, too." She would explain her motive later.

Four of the five sons understood Mama was doing what she always had, stepping in to shield them from Bubba. As adults, they wouldn't see or talk to her for weeks sometimes, but they still remembered the bruises she often carried when she stepped in on their behalf as teenagers. Junior was such a literal thinker, though, who took his mother's words to heart. That night, he drove his family home, put his children to bed, and told his wife he loved her before heading back to his shop in the backyard to work on a boat he was repairing for a friend. His wife was worried about Junior, but soon she saw the familiar flicker of his welding rod completing its work on his friend's project. An hour later, she heard the gunshot that ended his life.

Bubba Reynolds never shed a tear over Junior. He refused to let his wife attend the funeral of a coward. The other four sons wanted retribution on the old man, but the law didn't prohibit being a jerk. Martha blamed herself and looked for an escape hatch. She doubted she would find one while Bubba was still alive, and she couldn't bring herself to kill the man. A month after Junior's death, her injuries from the aftermath of Bubba's blowup with the boys had healed. She was once again allowed to go out in public, though never without Bubba. She was such a dutiful wife to an old tyrant, the locals said under their breaths and certainly never where Bubba could hear them.

Bubba walked out one morning after barely touching the enormous breakfast he always had her prepare. "I've got to deliver some hay," he growled.

She risked a question. "Who to, dear?"

He looked up with a snide smile. *Dear. She always comes back around. Just needs to be put in her place every now and again.* "Over to Country Joe Eady's place. No need to fix lunch today. Have supper ready early, though. I'll be plenty hungry."

Yeah, and plenty drunk. Country Joe Eady lived on the

other side of the county, but Bubba would drive his tractor and trailer full of hay over the main roads to deliver it. He would be shot the bird a dozen times today as he held up traffic from one end of the county to the other. Bubba Reynolds relished the thought of the negative attention. Heck, if he was behind his quota, he would slow down on purpose to "stir 'em up a bit."

As soon as Martha heard the tractor's diesel engine fire up, she made quick work of retrieving her small bag of clothes from under the pile of blankets and quilts in the hall closet. She wrapped several sausage and biscuits in aluminum foil and threw them in the bag, along with a thirty-two ounce Coke bottle full of water. Bubba had never allowed her to learn to drive, but she had convinced Jubal, the longtime farmhand Bubba employed, to teach her during previous Country Joe Eady days. Today's escape was a dry run in Jubal's truck. She would be back in plenty of time to have supper ready, but first she would navigate the back roads to the Pleasant Acres Cemetery to visit with her boy a spell.

After two successful dry runs over the next few months, Martha was prepared to make her escape. That's the only word she could conjure up to adequately describe what she meant to do. She laid the groundwork with months of gritting her teeth to be unusually sweet to Bubba, who became increasingly pompous with her. And careless. A month earlier, when she felt like she could wait no longer, she used a Country Joe Eady day to walk down by one of the ponds and pour out her sorrow to the Lord and make sure she wasn't going against Him. That was the last time she planned to be home when he returned from across the county.

The sun was beginning to set before she noticed the day getting away from her, and she panicked that Bubba would be home any time. When he walked in and supper wasn't ready, all of her humiliating preparation would be for naught. She felt a nudge in her spirit that reminded her of a tray of spaghetti she had hidden in the deep freeze for just such an occasion. She hurried home, threw it in the oven, and was melting cheese over the top of it when Bubba walked in the door, apparently sober.

"Hey, dear, how was your day at Country Joe's?"

"He's still as ornery as I am. You've got it smellin' good in here. What are we havin'?"

"Spaghetti. I just added the cheese, and the bread is ready to put in the oven. By the time you get cleaned up, it'll be ready to serve."

"Good." *Got her trained, that's for sure. Just had to put her in her place, show her who's boss.*

When Bubba had eaten two plates of spaghetti and a hearty slice of apple pie, he commented on the abundance of leftovers. That opened the door for Martha to ask about having the boys and their families over to help eat the rest of it on Sunday. She missed her grandbabies.

"That's what this is all about, huh?" After glaring at his wife for a solid minute and seeing a level of fear he deemed appropriate, he roared with laughter. "Sure, invite 'em over. I don't care. I'll come up with something for them to do to make up for their insolence last time."

Bubba never thought they would darken his door again—a bunch of weaklings, the whole lot of 'em. But he didn't reckon on a mother's power of persuasion. When the boys talked about it later, they agreed something in their mama's tone caused them to believe she was having thoughts of joining Junior.

RIGHT AFTER CHURCH ON SUNDAY, the boys and their families drove out to the farm. Junior and his family's absence was evident but unmentioned. Bubba enjoyed the tension for which he gave himself credit. What an evil, evil man, thought all the daughters-in-law. They kept their children—as well as any conversation they dared offer—close to the vest. Meanwhile, Martha finagled a private audience with one son after another and some of the older grandchildren. The girls, in particular, were haunted by her words: "My mother always told me to take my time and choose wisely when it came to choosing a husband. I didn't listen, but I beg you to pay attention to what I'm telling you. You cannot comprehend the hell I have been through by not heeding her advice. Please, please, please don't repeat my mistake."

Six weeks later, at eight-thirty on a Thursday morning, Bubba turned the corner on Lafell Road, where he and Martha lived, to take Country Joe Eady a trailer full of hay. Two minutes after, Martha pulled out of the driveway in the other direction in the GMC work truck she had bought from Jubal for a thousand carefully saved dollars on her way to a new life. Before she reached her new rental house in the old part of Harriston, she stopped at Junior's house, where the other sons handed her the keys and the paperwork for her new bank account. She kissed Junior's wife on the cheek and begged her forgiveness. She took the key from her oldest son and drove to her new home.

About the same time Martha was walking into her new home and her new life, Johnny Ray Willis pulled his Dodge pickup across the double yellow line near the top of Carter's Grade to make an ill-advised pass of a slower vehicle. He had almost completed his pass near the pinnacle of the hill when his vehicle plowed into the tractor coming up the hill in the middle of the road in the other direction. Bubba Reynolds' dead body landed thirty yards from the scene. Martha waited through the probate period and inherited everything her husband owned, and nobody was ever the wiser.

6

"Granny made a new life for herself here in Harriston. Nobody knew her here, or at least if they did, they didn't begrudge her a chance to start over. She never remarried, never even dated, as far as I can tell. She only told her story to her Sunday school class at a class prayer meeting one night, and that's how Mr. Jimmy Lee knew. Once I knew my granny's story, it made sense why my grandmother and mother never wanted much to do with her. Junior Reynolds was my mother's father, and she was three years old when he killed himself. Her mother never forgave Granny for my grandfather's death, even though Granny asked several times. And perhaps my fondness for my great-grandmother and her willingness to help me at my lowest point rubbed my mother the wrong way.

"Mom told me her father was cleaning his gun when it went off, and that's how he died. I never considered there might be more to the story than that. My mother became a by-product of her mother because Grandma passed her unforgiveness and bitterness down to Mom. My granny's story helped me learn more about who my mother is and to consider her a product of her past. She didn't just wake up one day and decide to be the way she is."

Pastor Hobbs spoke up. "How did you decide to approach the conversation with your mother, Tara?"

"I asked Mom to meet me for lunch at her favorite restaurant and told her I wanted to treat. I arrived first and picked a table in the back. She mumbled hello, sat down, and asked what I had done this time. The old me would have stood up and walked out on her. I was ready and prayed up, though. I told her the story Granny had shared with her Sunday school class and asked to hear her side of the story. She was taken aback that I knew Granny's story, but she told me what she understood from her mother's perspective. My grandmother died of cancer about two years ago, but Mom said before she died, Grandma told her the true story of what happened to her father. Grandma never talked to Granny about it again, though, even though she knew by then that she didn't have many more opportunities. She died with that bitterness still in her heart.

"Mom said that's probably why Granny wanted to help me, to make up for what she still felt like she unintentionally did to my grandfather. I asked Mom what Grandma was like when she was growing up. She immediately laughed in sort of a sarcastic way and said,

'Well, I can tell you this: there was certainly no pleasing that woman. Nothing I did was good enough for her, no ma'am.'

"And then she just stopped—I mean stopped cold when she realized she was describing herself. She put her hand over her mouth, and I jumped at my best opportunity to ask her forgiveness for the pain that I had caused her and our family. She started crying and nodded her head over and over. Then, she fell on her knees right there in the restaurant—where we were sitting, hardly anybody noticed, but still—and she apologized and begged my forgiveness for not being there for me. The epiphany of thinking only of herself on my darkest day crushed her. It was the closest I have ever felt to my mother."

"That's awesome," Pastor Hobbs said. "Did you talk to your brother?"

"John David still won't give me the time of day. He overheard Mom telling Dad about our conversation at the restaurant, and he got mad at me all over again. I guess I can see how he thinks I'm always dominating their attention, but I never did any of it to hurt him. Maybe he'll come around when he's older, but I feel like I did everything I could right now to patch things up with him."

"Good for you. There's a good chance he'll change his mind when he gets out on his own. Does he ever spend time with Zan?"

Tara smiled. "Yes, but he doesn't want me to know it. Dad has seen him teaching Zan to play ball, laughing with him and having a grand ol' time. Any time I'm around, though, he makes himself scarce, even from Zan. I think John David loves him and enjoys being an uncle, but admitting that would mean humbling himself to cultivate some kind of relationship with me. He's just not gonna do that right now.

"Long story maybe a little shorter, I received my one-year coin celebrating twelve months sober one week and the next week, another coin celebrating completion of the twelve steps. Since then, I've started leading a women's step study, and I'm sponsoring a young lady of my own now. My mom has come to CR with me for the last few weeks, too, to work through the unforgiveness she carried so long. She understands now that carrying her mother's offense affected how she mothered me. It sounds weird to say, but Celebrate Recovery has been the best mother-daughter time we have ever spent together. The best part of my year was when I regained custody of Zan with my parents' full support."

"Sounds like you've had quite a year," Austen said. "It might sound a little strange coming from someone you barely know, but I want you to know I'm so proud of you."

"Thank you," Tara answered, holding out both of her hands to take Austen's. Looking out at the rest of the group, she said, "And thank you, Lonesome, Party of Six. Knowing that we would be coming back here tonight and that you had such high hopes for me when I walked out that door last year, I seared your faces in my memory and imagined what they would look like if I strung together a year's worth of good choices. It was difficult sometimes, but I'll tell you, I'm looking around the room tonight seeing the same approving looks I had imagined, and I'm proud of my choices from the last twelve months. Thank you all very much."

JIMMY LEE

7

"**M**r. Jimmy Lee," Austen said, "you're next."

"So I am, so I am." Pops stood and walked to the front of the room, stopping for a hug from Tara.

He grinned and announced, "I've got the girl in church regular now, but she still can't keep her hands off of me." Everybody but James Junior laughed. He just shook his head.

"Last year," he began, "I was here because my son was sick. James Junior is here with me tonight because I told him all about you at least one time more than he wanted to hear. Since last year, I have been in touch with more of you than anybody else except maybe Laticia. Easton visited to do some fishing at my place in the country. We recognize how focused he gets on one thing at a time, right? Well, his improvement between his first fishing expedition and his second was remarkable."

Easton planted his face in his right hand as Pops continued. "Yep, he doubled his total on our second outing." Easton held up his left index finger, then added his middle finger. Pops laughed. "Yeah, but one of those two was a monster—must have gone twelve, thirteen… ounces."

As the group chuckled along with him, Pops grew serious. "Last Thanksgiving was a tough one for me, believing everybody had forgotten me. Fact was, I had fallen into such a routine that I wasn't putting myself out there to meet new people like I used to do. Thanksgiving changed all that. I've got a few folks I'd like to thank for that opportunity. First, the good Lord for giving me a ninety-third year. Last year, I wasn't so sure I wanted one, but it turned into one of the best years of my life, and that's saying something. I also want to thank James Junior for finding himself a little under the weather last year and my beautiful bride for not letting me feel sorry for myself.

"For those of you who don't know, my Catherine has been gone better than twenty years now, but I visit her nearly every day, and she keeps me straight. Even after all this time, I can predict how she would answer pretty much any question I throw at her. Last year she told me to try something different for Thanksgiving, and that's when I met all of you through Austen here.

"You guys might imagine after ninety-three years, I might be content to wait out my days and hope for a few when my body cooperates with the plans my mind makes. I want to tell you how I've been learning and growing and investing in others while we've made another trip around the sun. First thing I did was trim my neighbor's crepe myrtles and haul off the limbs for her. Y'all remember, she was the one that about talked my ears off last year while I was trying to get here. However, if she hadn't stopped me, I would have already eaten and gone before the rest of you arrived. The Lord reminded me of that the next day, so I trimmed Ethel's crepe myrtles and kept a respectful attitude about it. Full disclosure, I waited until she left for the beauty shop before I got started. She spends a solid three hours there every Friday, though for the life of me..."

"Dad..." James Junior interrupted.

"Right, right, don't go there." Pops laughed and continued, "Helping her was my first order of business. I waited two or three days before I told James Junior I had something I wanted to talk to him about. He was over his bug by then, and we returned to our routine of reading the paper together. I wanted to talk about my will, even though I wasn't planning on using it for a while. We both live simple lives and don't need for much but the paper in the morning, stout coffee, restaurants that will cook what we like, and the good Lord watching over us. Since I don't have any family past James Junior to consider, I was thinking about investing my money somewhere that would outlast either of us. He asked me how much I was talking about, and I pulled out my retirement account statements for him to see, and he just about passed out.

"I put back plenty to retire on, but I've always lived on less than I brought home, even my social security check. Plus, consider the number of extra years my investments have been earning interest after most people have already died. I told James Junior I wanted to split my money into fourths and start giving it away now. I wanted to give him a fourth and the general college scholarship fund at the college a fourth. The rest I wanted to split between the Janie Ruth Hobbs Scholarship Fund for West Cary High School and the homeless shelter where she served. Now, this is not something I want advertised around town, but that amounts to about a half million dollars apiece." The room filled with low whistles and then applause as the attendees stood to their feet.

"Hold on, let me brag on my kid for a minute," Pops said. "James Junior told me he was fine and didn't need my money. He did, however, come up with an idea I wish I had thought of myself. I'll wait until the end of my talk here to tell y'all about that one. First, though, I want to report on some other fishing trips I have enjoyed this year.

"I took Pastor Hobbs to a lake tucked behind some pine thickets near his church. He didn't even realize it existed, but I told y'all I have access to a bunch of fishing holes. Anyway, we had a good time and caught more fish than we wanted to clean. He had a lot of questions about being a widower, so I used my experience in that area to guide an enjoyable talk I hope has served him well.

"I took another fella fishing this year, the young man who cuts my grass now. I figured fifty-five years was long enough for James Junior to do it, although that's got to be some kind of world record for doing a chore. Let me say that if you live in Harriston and need some yard work done, David Gull & Associates gets two thumbs up from this old man." David smiled and waved at Pops. "However, he gets wrapped up in his company sometimes, so he needed some guidance for establishing a pattern of taking time off from work. Since nobody had ever taken him fishing before, I started him off at a honey hole no more than a dozen folks have fished in the last five years. It doesn't matter how inexperienced you are, you will catch all the fish you can handle there. David remarked what a beautiful day it would have been for cutting grass… right before a five-pound bass popped the first lure he threw in the water. Then, he was all about the fishing."

"So everybody caught a boatload of fish except me?" Easton asked.

"You didn't need to learn to catch fish. You needed to learn to love fishing. There's a difference. Plus, you caught more than Jeremiah."

"Facts," Jeremiah Turner asserted from the back of the room.

"Jeremiah and I never quite got around to flipping a lure in the water," Pops said. "When he walked up to my pond, I was tying a Carolina rig, but I could tell he didn't have much interest in fishing that day. He didn't bring any gear and didn't come dressed for a day at the pond. I pointed toward a pair of Adirondack chairs under a live oak tree not spittin' distance from the pond. I keep them there for when I want to sit and hear from God. Jeremiah sat in God's chair.

"I expected a flood of questions, but he just had one statement: 'Tell me about my great-grandfather.' When I asked him how long he had, he answered, 'As long as it takes.' I brought coffee, water and snacks, so I was prepared to stay as long as he wanted to talk, which turned out to be until late afternoon. I started with the first day I met my Jeremiah, near the spot we were sitting. That's one reason I keep up the place and still come out here at least once a week when the weather's nice. It gives me somewhere other than the graveyard to visit my friend."

8

"Hey, white boy." The little black boy at the barbed wire fence wore nothing but overalls and an ill-fitting straw hat.

"Hey, black boy." Jimmy Lee Yates had wandered from his pallet under the sprawling tree by the pond when his daddy took a walk to see if fish were biting on the other side. He was adorned in his usual cutoff blue jean shorts, white T-shirt, and rubber boots.

"I'm five."

"Me, too."

"I live over yonder." Black Boy turned his head toward the houses they could see in the distance.

"I live over the hill a piece." White Boy pointed in the opposite direction.

"What can you do?"

"I can fish."

"Me, too."

"I can bait my own hook."

"I've been doing that since I was three. My daddy wouldn't let me fish if I didn't."

"I can play catch."

"Me, too. You got a glove?"

"No, but my daddy does."

"My Uncle Joe got one. I can catch with my bare hands."

"I know my letters."

Jimmy Lee's boast was the trump card in a one-up conversation between a white boy and a black boy in rural south Mississippi in the early 1930s. The young black boy hung his head, ashamed.

"I can teach you sometime."

His head snapped up. "You wouldn't get in trouble?"

"Why would I get in trouble for teaching you your letters?"

"I don't know."

"What's your name?"

"Jeremiah. What's yours?"

"Jimmy Lee."

"Why you got two names?"

"I reckon because my mama and daddy wanted to call me two names. My daddy's got two names and a letter. Why do you reckon you got one name?"

"Probably too no account for more than one."

"Why are you no account?"

Jeremiah hung his head again. "I don't know."

"You want me to teach you a letter?"

"I reckon."

Jimmy Lee picked up a stick and wrote a capital *E*

and a lowercase e in the dirt between him and his new friend. "This is *e*, the letter in my daddy's name."

"Why he got a letter?"

"His full name is Robert E. Lee Yates. The *E* don't stand for anything."

"Why it's in there then?"

"I reckon it was his mama and daddy's favorite letter or something."

"I wish I had another name, or at least a letter. My name is just Jeremiah Johnson. Ain't got no middle name."

"That's weird. Anyway, this is *e*. Sometimes it makes an e sound, like the letter, and sometimes you say it *eh*."

"Why come they say it like that?"

"They just do."

"How are you supposed to figure out how to say it?"

"Beats me. My mama tells me which way to say it when we get to a word I don't know."

"And you gonna tell me?"

"Sure, I will."

"It sounds like letters is hard."

"Not if you work on it."

"I ain't scared of work. Show me a word with an *e* in it."

"I can't write words yet, but I'll ask my mama. Tree has a *e* in it. Tr-ee. Hear it?"

"Yeah. What letter makes the *tr* sound?"

"I'll ask my mama. Bed has a *e* in it, too. Buh-eh-duh. Listen to it in the middle. Buh-eh-duh."

"Letters still seem like they is hard."

Jimmy Lee puffed up with pride. "Oh, they're not too bad if you put your mind to it."

"And you for real gonna teach me? I'll put my mind to it, I promise."

"Sure, I will. I'll be a good teacher."

Just then, Robert E. Lee Yates yelled for his son from across the pond. "Jimmy Lee, where you at, boy?" Jeremiah crouched in fright.

Jimmy Lee said, "I'll be right back." He poked his head around the tree and yelled back, "I've got to pee!"

"All right, go ahead! Don't wander off!"

"I won't!"

Five-year-old Jimmy Lee trotted back to the fence. "I better pee, so I'm not telling a lie."

"I gotta go, too. Wanna cross?"

"Sure." Both boys dropped their underwear to their ankles and crossed streams of urine, a sure sign of solidarity. They giggled and returned their clothing to its previous state.

"Hey, Jimmy Lee, can you keep a secret?"

"Cross my heart and hope to die."

"I mean, can you keep our teaching a secret? I want to learn my letters, but my mama and daddy—they never learned 'em, and I want to surprise 'em when I learn mine."

"Okay, it'll be our secret."

"Can you come here anytime you want?"

"Sure, I can," Jimmy Lee lied. If his mama had said it once, she had told him a thousand times not to go near the pond by himself. *If I go way around the pond, I won't be lying to Mama.*

"They's too many of us children for mama to keep up with, so I can come tomorrow afternoon."

"Okay. My mama makes me lay down on a pallet under the tree in the backyard while she takes a nap inside. I stay down till she's had long enough to go to sleep, and then I do whatever I want. I'll come here and bring one of my learning books with me."

"See you tomorrow, Jimmy Lee."

"See you tomorrow, Jeremiah."

"We met for the better part of two years with nobody paying enough attention to catch us—not that we believed we were doing anything that needed hiding. It was more adventurous to meet in secret, though, so we didn't tell anybody. Jeremiah and me both became solid readers because of all our practice. Mama let me go fishing by myself when I turned six, so I took off for the pond about every afternoon. I would take my readers and tell her I was practicing my reading when I took a break from fishing. That made her happy, and it made my daddy happy when I would sometimes bring back enough fish for supper. With so many brothers and sisters and cousins running around their little cluster of houses backed up to our property, nobody ever noticed Jeremiah missing.

"One day when Jeremiah and I were both seven, my mama needed me for something, and she came looking for me. It was during the spring when the leaves were still damp from a morning shower. We didn't notice her coming until she was close enough to lay eyes on us. Even though she was polite, her face revealed panic. She asked me to introduce her to my little friend. I did, and she was nice to him, but she said I needed to come with her to the house right away. I told Jeremiah I would see him the next day and walked off with Mama.

"As soon as we were out of sight, she pulled me behind a big sycamore and asked me what I thought I was doing. I told her about teaching my friend Jeremiah to read. He read as well as me after two years of lessons, but we kept up our studying like we always had. Only now, instead of me teaching him something I learned months ago, I taught him what Mama had taught me a day or two before. Mama asked me if I had told Daddy about Jeremiah, but then she mumbled, 'Of course not.' She got a look on her face I recognize today as defiance. 'Tell you what,' she said, 'Your daddy might not understand, so let's not tell him, okay?' I told her I would explain it to him, but she seemed dead set on keeping it from my father. She was my mama and the most important person in the world to me, so I trusted her and played along with what she said.

"I asked her if that meant Jeremiah and I needed to stop reading together. I remember she sucked in the right side of her lip. That meant you didn't argue with her. This time, though, she didn't seem to aim her sneer at me. I didn't notice anything my daddy had done to get on her bad side, but whatever she had in mind was getting back at him somehow.

"'No, Jimmy Lee, I'll tell you what we'll do. You like adventures, right?' I assured her I did. 'Well, you know that gigantic magnolia tree on the far side the pond? I want you and Jeremiah to do your lessons in there where nobody can see you from the outside world. It will be like y'all's little kingdom in there. I've got an old bench in the back of the barn that y'all can sit on—won't nobody miss it. Would the two of you like that?'

"I told her I thought Jeremiah and I would have big times doing adventure learning. And we did, too. Sometimes, Mama would sneak snacks in my britches' pocket for Jeremiah and me to enjoy during our school. Every so often, she would remind me to be quiet if we heard Daddy coming and especially if he was working in the pasture on the other side of the hill. She said if he ever called me and wondered what I was doing in there.... That's when I cut her off and told her I would tell him I was doing number two. She laughed and said that would work. I didn't understand why we were being so secretive, but I enjoyed playing along.

"Mama's plan worked fine for the next month, but one day Daddy came back from the fields in the middle of the afternoon looking for me. Mama told him I had gone fishing. He grabbed his pole and came to the pond to join me. Jeremiah and I had finished our reading lesson inside our canopy hideout, and we were laughing about something when Daddy heard us. He hollered for me, and I came out from our hiding place while Jeremiah sneaked out the back way. Daddy asked what I was doing in there and why I didn't come when he first called me. I told him I needed to poop and wasn't finished wiping with leaves when he hollered for me. At first he looked suspicious, but he just sort of giggled. He walked away, but he stopped to ask me what I was laughing so hard about in there.

"I reached for any reason on the spur of the moment, so I told him Willie had told a funny joke. Willie was my imaginary friend from earlier in my childhood. Daddy said that five years old was too old to have pretend friends anymore, so he made me pretend Willie had moved away. I hadn't thought about him much since, but he seemed a convenient excuse. Daddy believed me. He scolded me for not minding him to get rid of my imaginary friend two years before, but his heart wasn't in it. I overheard him laughing when he told Mama about it later. I figured Mama would be proud of me for coming up with such a good one.

"It turned out Daddy doubted my explanation. He searched inside the magnolia tree while I was reading with Mama one morning. Our bench and markings on the ground revealed more than pooping going on in there. Later that week, Daddy informed Mama at lunch that he was going into town and wouldn't be back until supper time. I loved days like that because Jeremiah and I could fish without having to worry about Daddy's coming up on us all of a sudden. Sneaking up on us was what he had in mind, though."

9

"**J** ames. Lee. Yates." It was Jimmy Lee's in trouble name. His father's tone was cold as he appeared seemingly out of nowhere. It sent shivers through Jimmy Lee.

"Hey, Daddy. This is my friend Jeremiah." Pulling the stringer from the water, he said, "Look, we've caught four good ones already."

"I see." His face had not brightened one iota. Turning to Jeremiah, he said, "Boy, I believe it's high time you hightailed it on home." Jeremiah backed up two steps, his eyes unable to unlock from the hatred in Robert E. Lee Yates's eyes. "Now, boy, git!" Jeremiah sprinted toward the strands of barbed wire separating the properties, slid under them, and never checked up until he was out of sight.

"Daddy, why did you..."

Robert E. Lee Yates cut off his son's question with controlled rage. "I'll do the talking and you'll do the listening. You lied to me about being in the tree by your-self." He fumed as he repeated, "You lied to me."

Jimmy Lee dropped his head, guilty. "I did, Daddy. I'm sorry." He didn't understand the unmistakable hatred in his daddy's eyes. He comprehended at some deep level that his friendship with Jeremiah was taboo, but his mama didn't want to tell him why. Right then, he didn't feel safe and wondered if he showed deep contrition over the deception, it might diffuse the situation. He dared not confront his daddy over Robert Yates's rudeness to his friend. He mumbled beneath his breath.

"What did you say, boy? Speak up!"

"I-I was just saying that-that…" His lip quivered uncontrollably now. "… that I was trying to have ad-adventures like-like the ones I s-sometimes read about."

"That's what this was? Adventures?" Perhaps Daddy was remembering his own experiences on this land as a youngster, Jimmy Lee hoped. "How long you friendly with this boy?"

"A little while. We have adventures in the tree." His father softened the least bit. "D-do you want to come s-see our fort? You might could fit in it." He and Jeremiah had swept their 'tablet' clean with a pine branch they used as an eraser for their dirt chalkboard.

"You telling me the truth this time?"

"Y-yes, Daddy."

"That boy just part of your adventures?"

"Yes, sir. If he's good, I let him fish in our pond, but he wouldn't take any of the fish. I was going to bring them all home to you and surprise you," Jimmy Lee lied. He and Jeremiah always split their catch fifty-fifty, no strings attached.

"If he's good, huh?"

"He's been real good lately." Jimmy Lee didn't comprehend why he said that, but it seemed to take away the last of his daddy's anger, so he kept going in that direction. He made a mental note to ask his mama about it in private later and to apologize if what he said would hurt Jeremiah. He wondered if Jeremiah would ever return to their meeting spot.

On Sunday, though, when several days had passed like normal—sans Jeremiah—Jimmy Lee missed his friend enough to broach the subject.

"Daddy, can I ask you a question?"

"Son, you need to get ready for church."

"I'm ready, Daddy. I got up extra early today."

Robert Yates looked down at his son, noticing him this time. "So you are, son. What do you need?"

"Daddy, could I—maybe sometime—invite Jeremiah to come to church with us?"

The color drained from Jimmy Lee's daddy's face, and he realized his question had crossed some kind of line. "Son, we need to have us a talk after we get back home today. I don't have time right now. I have a deacon's meeting before church this morning. But to answer your question, the answer is no."

"Why not, Daddy? Jeremiah is my friend."

"Son, my answer is no. And that's final. Do not ask me again. We'll talk about it this afternoon."

"Daddy?"

"Don't ask me again, son."

"I won't, Daddy. Can I ask you something else?"

Robert grunted. "What is it?"

"Are you mad at me? Did I do something wrong?"

Jimmy Lee's father reached down and tussled his son's hair. "No, son, I'm not angry with you. You just don't understand how the world works yet. We'll work on that this afternoon."

THE CHURCH SERVICE passed more slowly than usual for Jimmy Lee that Sunday. His daddy didn't act mad at him anymore, but he couldn't shake the feeling he had done something wrong. The preacher was fired up this Sunday, pounding his fist on the pulpit as he railed against sin. Jimmy Lee sat still like he had been trained. When the Lord was in His holy temple, all the earth—especially seven-year-old boys—should be silent… and still. This morning, every fiber of his being itched. When the small congregation sang the final amen, Jimmy Lee bolted past the circle of smokers starting to gather in front of the church and attacked his itches.

Sunday lunch was no easier for Jimmy Lee. Mama's fried chicken was his favorite, but he didn't muster much of an appetite. Daddy seemed more friendly than usual to both of them, and Jimmy Lee couldn't figure out why. As the time ticked deliberately toward "we'll work on that this afternoon," his uneasiness increased to where his stomach cramped. Just as he was ready to race to the outhouse, Daddy looked his way and said,

"Son, grab your fishing pole, and let's walk back to the pond."

Perhaps he forgot, Jimmy Lee hoped as they walked toward the fishing hole. They hadn't dug in Mama's flower beds for worms, though, so his hopes weren't high. As soon as they reached the pond, Robert E. Lee Yates pointed toward two stumps they used for their occasional father-son talks and set his fishing pole on the ground. "Have a seat, son. Let's talk about you and your little nigger friend."

There it was. Jimmy Lee didn't understand much about his daddy's actions from the last few days, but that word he understood. Daddy used it often, and Mama scolded him for it, but it only seemed to encourage him to say it more. The grownup men at church used the word all the time, but Daddy's use of it registered as personal. This was his friend. Jeremiah's skin was black, but Jimmy Lee never thought of him as a *nigger*.

"Son, let me give you a lesson about the way things work. Back in the olden days, as you kids like to say, white men brought niggers to this country to work the cotton fields here in the South. Some uppity folks up north got the idea they should be free, but they didn't depend on 'em like we did down here. So the South broke away from the North so we could live like we saw fit. That was called the Civil War. You ever heard of that?"

"Yes, sir."

"Well, it was the War of Northern Aggression, if you ask anybody from the South back in those days. We broke off and started our own country, the Confederate States of America. There's a lot of folks that believe the South is gonna rise again one day, and I'm one of 'em. There was slavery in the Bible, so we don't see nothing wrong with it. Here in Miss'ippi, we joined up with other states to write new laws to keep niggers in their place until then. Niggers got their public bathrooms; we got our'n. Niggers got their own schools; we got our'n. Niggers got their own drinkin' fountains; we got our'n. You understand what I'm talking about, son?"

"Yes, sir, but..." Jimmy Lee cringed each time his daddy said the word.

"Hold on, let me finish. So we got these laws that keep whites and niggers separate. We got operations in place so they know their place."

"Like what?"

For the first time, Robert Yates hesitated. Jimmy Lee caught it, but his father followed the brief pause with the cruel gaze he had given Jeremiah the day he sent him away. "Boy, I guess you're gonna figger things out eventually, so you might as well know now. Worst thing the white man can do these days is allow niggers to vote. There's places in Miss'ippi where there's more of them than us. Can you imagine what it would be like if they started votin' their own kind into office? No, I reckon you can't. But you just take my word for it, we've got to do ever'thing in our power to make sure that doesn't happen." He broke off his diatribe for a moment, glaring into the distance with a smirk on his face.

Jimmy Lee muddled into the break. "Daddy, what do

you mean, 'everything in our power'?" He feared the answer.

"Keep 'em from gettin' into the votin' booths. Make it hard for 'em to vote by makin' 'em pass readin' tests and such. Most of 'em are too stupid to read, anyhow, but we can rig the tests to make it harder for 'em to pass. If they're bound and determined to put their names on the rolls, we got other ways to encourage 'em not to." More hesitance to go further as he looked away.

"Like what?"

Robert E. Lee Yates whirled to stare deep into his small son's eyes. His teeth were clenched, and Jimmy Lee drew back from the cruelty of the devil himself. "Like the Ku Klux Klan, son. Like burnin' crosses in niggers' yards. Intimidation, boy, that's how the white man keeps power. If that don't keep 'em down, we string one of 'em up so they'll see what happens if they don't stay in line. So you listen to me good, son, if you know what's good for you. You stop hanging around with that little nigger boy before he gets himself made an example of, you hear me?"

10

The room stood dead silent as Pops fought back tears eighty-six years after the fact. "I wanted to cry, but I determined at seven years old to defy everything that hateful man said. I refused to cry because he thought I would. He stood to head back toward the house, but he growled that I should consider what he'd said before I took up with that 'darky' again. As soon as he topped the hill and was out of sight, I vomited. I thought about what he said and heaved until nothing remained inside of me. I lay on the ground, listening to Mama and Daddy yelling so loudly at one another that I heard them clear down to the pond. At least I knew where he was.

"Something happened while I lay on the ground that is still so clear in my mind, it seemed like it happened yesterday. I felt a light touch on my shoulder, and a gentle voice asked, 'Jimmy Lee, you okay?' Jeremiah circled back and hid inside the magnolia tree throughout my father's tirade. I could tell it frightened him, but he came out to check on me, anyway. I jumped up and hugged him and told him he would be my friend forever, no matter what. And he was.

He pointed to Jeremiah Turner sitting with his brother and their wives. "Until I shared that story with this Jeremiah, I hadn't told anybody but my mama and James Junior. I told Junior the night before I told Jeremiah—thought he ought to understand why I never wanted him to know much about his grandfather. He seemed to have an idea already. Guess it's the journalist in him. Say, how *did* you know, son?"

"The ornament."

"You've seen it?" James Junior nodded.

"Dang you, Bruce," Pops muttered.

Easton voiced the curiosity of the rest of the room. "Now that you've told the story, you want to tell us about the ornament?"

Pops nodded. "I left home between Thanksgiving and Christmas for boot camp as soon as I could get out from under that man. I was an only child, so Mama made me a special ornament every year. Daddy knew she was making me one to take with me so I would think of her while I was gone. Daddy had heard about black men returning from the war saying if the government could integrate the army, then they should integrate the general population when they came back. So he made me his own ornament that year so I would remember what he had told me those years before down at the pond. It was a handmade and hand-painted Confederate flag.

"He waited until Mama had given me her little ornament to remember her by before he gave me his. Plus, he made me promise that I would always put it on my tree. I kind of nodded and reached to put it in my bag, but he grabbed my arm and looked me in the eye and said, 'Promise.' I promised. If I hadn't, Mama would have caught the brunt of whatever animosity I left behind. 'I promise' are the last words I ever spoke to my daddy. He died of a massive heart attack after I had been in the service about a year. The army had deployed me overseas, and I was relieved I didn't have to attend his funeral. I felt bad for my mama, though, even though she was free from him.

"Maybe it's stupid, but I have kept that promise to my daddy since 'I promise' were the final words I ever said to him. The ornament is faded to where it's hard to tell what it looked like when he made it. But every year I place it on the tree, I remember where I came from and thank God I've made a difference in the way this world looks at people. We haven't arrived as a people yet, but I can look at that little handmade ornament made from the hate of one man's heart and pride myself that I stopped that hate in my family in my generation."

"So… who is Bruce?" Easton asked.

James Junior snorted, which filled the room with tentative laughter. "My father names his Christmas trees. He calls the one he has now *Bruce Spruce*, and Dad talks to it like it's an actual person. What Dad didn't tell y'all is that he puts that ornament on the tree every year, but he puts it so deep inside Bruce that nobody ever sees it. Dang, Dad, you've got me calling him by name, too. I leaned over to put a present under the tree one year when I looked up and caught a glimpse of it. I saw Grandpa's name on the back. That was five or six years ago. I've known about Grandpa a lot longer than that, but enough about him. Dad, don't forget to tell them how you're spending my inheritance."

"Oh, yes, I almost forgot. Folks, with James Junior's help and with his blessing, we will establish the Jeremiah Johnson Memorial Scholarship for worthy students from mixed-race families in this area." After another round of applause, Pops continued. "My friend Jeremiah became the first in his family to learn to read. His daddy accused him of getting above his raising and putting them all in danger from a white man they recognized as part of the Klan. His brothers and sisters were jealous of him for being able to read. Jeremiah's mama was proud of him, though, and encouraged him. He finished high school and would have gone to college if he could have afforded it. For most of his life, he worked two jobs and sent all four of his own children to college. From what Carol told us about Isaiah and Jeremiah's mama—my Jeremiah's granddaughter—she's a very intelligent woman with a love for reading, too. Jeremiah changed his family tree, and I want to help other people like him go to school and make the most of themselves."

"Pops—Mr. Jimmy Lee—you came in here last year lonely and feeling like your life didn't have much meaning anymore," Easton said. "You've done more in this last year to impact future generations than the rest of us put together."

James Junior stood. "If I might have a minute, I would like to tell you a quick story I've never told my dad. It's how I knew about Grandpa." He looked at Pops, who nodded and shuffled back to his seat.

"WHEN I WAS sixteen years old, Pops dropped me off at the farm to spend a few weeks with Grandma. I had spent a week with her during the summer for most of my life, but once I turned thirteen, I thought I was too old to keep doing it. He kept making me go, though. The summer when I was sixteen, though, Grandma had fallen and broken her hip, and she needed more help around the house than Pops had time to give her. Her garden was coming in, so he volunteered me to pick and shell. Pops came in the evenings to blanch the vegetables to freeze for the winter. As a sixteen-year-old boy, I've got to tell you it wasn't my favorite idea for how to spend a summer. But I remember it now as one of the most meaningful times in my life.

"I would get up in the mornings and fix breakfast for Grandma. She ate oatmeal with pecans and raisins every day. Even though I tired of fixing her breakfast by day two and of eating it by day three, I sat by her bed, where we ate together and talked. I was about as interested in her stories as the typical teenager, thinking more about finishing my time on the farm than what Grandma had to say. I would tend the garden until noon, when she would fix sandwiches and potato chips. Grandma liked these lemon cookies that are still some of my favorites, and we ate more of those than we should have. I shelled peas and butter beans after lunch. Grandma wanted me to sit in her room while I shelled so she could help and tell me more stories.

"About the third day I was there, Grandma realized my heart wasn't in my work. We had been shelling for about thirty minutes when she asked, 'Does Jimmy Lee ever talk about his daddy?' I told her all I knew about Grandpa was that he farmed for a living and owned some office buildings in town, and he died of a heart attack when Pops was in the army."

"Do you respect your dad?"

"I guess, why?"

"James Junior, let me tell you about your grandfather. He was the most cruel man I ever met. He was a womanizer and a racist, and he tried his dead level best to get your daddy to be those things, too."

"Why did you marry him if he was like that, Grandma?"

She didn't answer for the longest time. When James Junior glanced over to make sure she was okay, he saw a tear trickling down her cheek. "I'm sorry, Grandma, I didn't mean to hurt your feelings."

"It's okay, Junior. It's a legitimate question, one I have asked myself many times through the years. No one else has ever been brave enough to ask. Thank you for that. I'm going to answer your question."

James Junior put his pan of peas on the floor next to the brown grocery bag where he was throwing the hulls. He reached over and touched his grandmother on the arm. She patted his hand and took a deep breath.

"When I was almost your age, automobiles fascinated me. Not many people in Harriston County owned a car in those days. Most people still drove horses and buggies. I mean, when the Depression hit this area not too long after we married, you couldn't tell a lot of difference because nobody had much to begin with. Your grandpa had money, though. He was older, twenty-five, ten years older than me, handsome. He noticed me looking at his Model A one Saturday when all the folks had come to town. When he asked me if I wanted to go for a ride in it, I didn't think twice. Although he was so much older than me, my parents didn't think twice about that. They saw a splendid opportunity for me to have things better than they did, maybe even be able to help them in their old age. I married Robert two months later—fifteen, married, and clueless about the ways of the world. I learned in a hurry."

"Wh-what happened, Grandma?" Junior returned his pan to his lap to give his nervous fingers something to do.

She considered whether James Junior was ready to hear ill of his own family.

"It's okay. I have already figured out Grandpa wasn't somebody I want to look up to. I'm okay with that, but I would like to understand why."

"All right, dear, here goes. Your grandfather's father owned an enormous farm, way bigger that what you or your daddy ever recognized as ours. Even though he couldn't own slaves as his father had before him, it wasn't much different. He had a bunch of sharecroppers who worked the land for him. They were almost all black, and they lived in these little shacks that Robert's father built. They weren't fit to live in because they didn't do much to keep the heat out in the summer or the cold in the winter.

"He practiced what many plantation farmers in the South did back then. He would charge them so much rent for those shacks that they couldn't possibly put back any money to buy a decent place of their own. Robert set up a little store on the property where they bought their necessities. He charged them whatever it took to keep them going—barely. When times were good, he'd raise the prices in the store so they never gained any forward momentum. When times were bad, he'd drop his prices just enough to encourage those poor souls to keep going.

"Robert's father died of scarlet fever when Robert was eighteen years old. His mother sold about a third of the place right away in order to pay the bills for a while. Robert had been working with his daddy for several years by then and saw how he kept all those poor share-croppers in line. He took it a step further. With a third less land and the same number of folks trying to make a living off the place, you might think he would turn some of them loose to find other places to farm. No, he told them that they needed to tighten their belts and get by on less. He gave them hope that one day he would buy back his daddy's land and then they'd all have it made.

"Those poor folks believed him. They worked hard for him for the first year, and Robert could have bought that land back. Instead, he bought up buildings in town and started increasing the rent on the businesses in them. And he bought that car. That stupid car. When he bought it, the sharecroppers figured he had sold them a bill of goods. And there I stood, fifteen years old and fascinated by that car. Oh, Junior, I have wished a million times I had never seen it.

"Anyway, we got married, and that's a big step for any girl, much less a teenager marrying a man in his twenties. He had learned the ways of the world, and I was naïve. I got busy setting up house, learning to cook the things he liked. One thing he would not allow is any of his hired folks to cook for him. We had two maids in the house, but he feared if they cooked the food, one of them might try to poison him. It didn't occur to me until later that he had been just fine with their cooking before he brought me home. Sadie and Harriet—those were the two maids—I got along fine with them. They taught me how to cook all of Robert's favorites—fried chicken, mashed potatoes with a few little chunks, the perfect shade of light brown gravy, biscuits with plenty of butter. At first, they cooked and I watched, but eventually, I got the hang of it.

"I had been there a month when I started asking Sadie and Harriet personal questions. They seemed reluctant to talk to me much at first—too concerned they were going to get in trouble with Mr. Robert, as they called him. They finally trusted me enough to tell me about their families, who worked on the farm. When I asked them where they lived, they looked at each other and exchanged this glance I didn't understand.

I pressed them to tell me, though, and Sadie finally answered.

"MRS. 'LIZBETH, ain't Mr. Robert ever showed you his place here?'"

"You mean the farm?"

"The farm ain't all 'bout fields, ma'am. They's the fields, yeah, but ain't he showed you the sto' and where the peoples live?"

"We have a store on the property?" I probably asked this with too much excitement because they stopped me right off.

"Not the kinda stores you go to in town, Mrs. 'Lizbeth. Not that kinda store a'tall. Tell you what, ma'am, one of these days when Mr. Robert goes on him a trip, we'll take you down there to where we stays. Then you'll understand."

"ABOUT A MONTH LATER, Robert told me he was going to Jackson for a few days to talk to some legislators. He asked if I would be all right staying at the farm by myself, but he didn't ask as if I had a choice. I told him I'd be fine. His mother still lived in a wing of the house she had all to herself, so she was there if I needed anything. Robert had a foreman who took care of everything on the farm anyway, so there was nothing I needed to do. Actually, with him not there to cook for, I had even less work than usual. Sadie cooked for his mama already over in her kitchen. I don't guess Robert worried much about the house servants poisoning her.

"As soon as his car puttered around the corner up the road from the house, I started asking Sadie and Harriet for a tour of the place. They told me I had better wait, that sometimes Mr. Robert forgot things and had to come back to the house for them. I came to understand later that he enjoyed trying to catch anybody who might get out of line. Sure enough, that day he burst through the door about an hour after he left to find Harriet and Sadie cleaning and me sewing up one of his socks that needed mending. He mumbled something about wanting his brown britches, and he strolled back out the door and drove around the bend five minutes later."

11

"We can go now," Harriet said. "He ain't ever come back more than once unless somebody's been outta line."

The dusty road that led from the house to the fields beckoned the nervous three women, who surveyed their surroundings before stepping onto the road. They had walked almost a mile when Elizabeth asked, "Y'all walk this far to work every day?" She noticed Harriet and Sadie exchange a glance.

"Mrs. Elizabeth, we only halfway there," Harriet informed her.

"Oh." Elizabeth remained silent for the rest of their walk, but she was taking in the surrounding activity. Sharecroppers in groups worked portions of the fields on both sides of the road as they passed by. It was fall, and the cotton crop was just beginning to come in, and they were working hard to stay ahead of it. Within a week, they would work from sunup to sundown and still not finish. Few of the workers glanced up as the white mistress walked the dusty road with the housemaids.

Elizabeth's right foot hinted the makings of a blister when she noticed the first ramshackle building. It was scarcely big enough to consider a house. She was ready for a break and hoping it was Harriet's or Sadie's house. "Whose house is that?"

After another flash of their eyes, Harriet answered, "Mrs. Elizabeth, I'm not sure what you was expectin', but that ain't no house. That's the sto'. Told you it ain't like the ones you's used to in town. We can go in if you want."

"Let's do that. I'll treat you to a Coke."

"No ma'am, I'm afraid you can't do that. I'm tellin' you, it ain't like the sto' in town."

"She better just see it for herself," Sadie chimed in. "Come on, Mrs. Elizabeth, check out what the nigger sto' look like."

"Please don't use that word, Sadie."

Sadie laughed. "You married to Robert E. Lee Yates and don't like that word? Ma'am, don't think me outta line when I say you'd better get good and used to it 'round here. Come on up inside the sto'."

"Howdy, Miss Sadie, Miss Harriet. Who's this y'all got with you today?" asked the colored man behind the counter. He was portly and wore wire-rimmed glasses too small for his face.

"This here's Mrs. Elizabeth, Mr. Robert's new wife. Mrs. Elizabeth, this here's Hiram. He run the sto' for Mr. Robert."

Hiram snorted, "She don't seem to me like she old enough marry Mr. Robert or anybody else. She look like a child herself."

Elizabeth found it odd that Hiram would talk about her as if she wasn't even there. Her attention moved toward the contents of the store. Sadie was right—it didn't resemble any other store she had ever entered. It was filled with farming equipment—smaller tools like hoes and seed sowers with plows in the back two corners. She had never seen an unattached plow before, and these two seemed rather lonely sitting in the corners.

Elizabeth wandered away from the counter toward the back of the store. Along the back wall, she found sacks of meal, flour, and sugar. The side wall featured bolts of cloth and a variety of hardware. The middle of the floor was empty except for a few farm implements she didn't recognize. "Harriet, where do you go if you need something you can't find at your store?"

Hiram joined the exchange of stares between Harriet and Sadie. "Ma'am," he said, "I got everything these folks need. If I ain't got it, they don't need it. And that's straight from yo' husband's mouth. He's the boss of me, so that's what goes. You'll find a sharecropper's family can make stuff go a lot farther than most folks. They ain't got no choice."

"But... I don't see any candy in the store. Can't the mamas treat their kids to a piece of candy every once in a while?"

"These younguns wouldn't know what candy is it wadn't for Mrs. Yates sneaking some out here ever now and again. Colored mamas put a little extra sugar in the biscuits sometimes, though. That's 'bout all the treats our children gets," Sadie said.

"Wait, you have children?"

Sadie threw back her shoulders. "Yes, ma'am, three of 'em: Jenny, Leroy, and Alvin, Jr. They's twelve, ten, and nine."

"Oh my gosh, I didn't realize you had children. My goodness, you're already at the house cooking for Robert's mama when I get up in the morning, and you don't go home until you've cleaned up after our dinner. When do you spend time with your kids?"

"I sees 'em in the mornin' times when they's up doin' they chores. I help 'em out sometimes. Alvin says I's spoilin' 'em, but a mama's gotta make time to spend with her chil'ren, don't she? We can go by and let you meet 'em."

"What time does their school end?"

The three colored folks swapped another glance. The volume of the exchanges agitated Elizabeth. Harriet noticed and pulled her by the arm toward the door. "Come on outside, honey, and we'll finish showin' you around."

"Come on, y'all, I'm well aware I don't understand the way things work, but y'all have got to stop with the secret looks. I want to know about your lives, but you keep cutting me off every time I ask a question. Now, start being upfront with me. You don't need to be afraid of me."

Harriet stayed silent while they walked, her hand on Elizabeth's arm, moving the teenager forward. When they had walked around a bend a quarter mile down the road, she pointed toward a group of stumps sitting under a grove of shade trees. "This here's where a lot of the nig—sorry, colored folks—come to eat lunch when they're anywhere close. It's the best shade on the entire property. We ain't got long if we gon' sneak 'round the houses before the women start fixin' lunch, so I'll make this quick."

"You sure you want the truth 'bout the way things operate 'round here? I believe we can trust you, but you got to understand that some folks—lots of folks—here ain't much more than slaves."

"But why?"

Harriet hesitated, but Sadie said, "Tell her."

Harriet nodded. "Because of the way yo' husband run this place, Mrs. Elizabeth."

"Robert?"

"You got another husband somewhere, Mrs. Elizabeth?" Sadie shot Harriet a stern gaze, but Elizabeth laughed.

"No, just the one. I'm getting the feeling there's a lot about him I don't understand."

"Yes, ma'am."

"Go on."

"All right, I'll go on, but you gots to promise what we tell you won't come back on us. You promise, Mrs. Elizabeth?"

"Okay, if you promise to do something for me. My family and friends call me *Liz*, and I wish y'all would, too. Robert calls me Elizabeth, says it makes me seem older, but I don't like it. Y'all can call me whatever you need to in front of him, but I would like to think we're friends, and my friends call me *Liz*." Harriet and Sadie nodded. "Okay, tell me what I'm not seeing around this place."

"We'll do you one better than that," Sadie said. "We'll tell you *and* show you. Back yonder at the sto', we had to hustle you outta there so's Hiram didn't hear nothing he would have to tell on you for. He's probly gonna tell Mr. Robert you was down there in the first place, but I'll try to git him not to. He Mr. Robert's snitch down here in the quarters. Somebody got some-thin' bad to say 'bout Mr. Robert, they better not say it 'round Hiram."

"Oh, if you can get him to not tell Robert about my tour of the place, I would appreciate it."

"I figure I'll make him a cake at the big house to take home to him. That outta do it. Hiram's my daddy and we stay at the same house. It's the biggest one in the quarters because Mr. Robert always take care of his snitches. 'Gotta keep 'em in line,' I always hear him sayin' to Hiram like he not one of 'em. My daddy got a plan to git us outta here one of these days, though. If Mr. Robert knew how much he was puttin' back to buy a place for all of us, he wouldn't pay him what he does. Now, Mrs. Elizabeth—Mrs. Liz…"

"Just *Liz*, please. And you don't have to worry about me telling. Keep going."

"That sto' ain't like what most sharecroppers got either on they plantation or in town. Most of those places got stuff like sweets and cheese, different meats. Mr. Robert, he give us what we needs to survive, but it ain't nothin' extra. We shuffle cakes and pies outta Mrs. Yates's little kitchen when we can. She'll flat go up in that house and distract Mr. Robert so we's can smuggle stuff outta there sometimes. She notice what he doin' and she don't like it much, neither, she don't. The folks down here in the quarters—there's the houses up ahead —they stay around for two reasons. One, they love Mrs. Yates and feel loyal for all the stuff she done smuggled down here all these years. And two, Mr. Robert makes sure don't nobody get through the year without owin' him money at the end."

"How do they owe him money when they work so hard?"

"Ain't about how hard somebody work out here. Ever'thing you get at the sto' back yonder go against the crops you bring in. You need anything from a shovel to a mule to a cow to chickens—Mr. Robert make sure you git 'em. You don't pay for that stuff, neither; it go on yo' credit at the sto'. You pay off your credit at harvest time with a cut of the crops. Don't matter how good a year you have with cotton or corn or beans, neither. Long as he keepin' the books at the sto', you always gon' finish the year owin' a little more than you gits. Then you gots to work another year for Mr. Robert. That make sense to you?"

Liz's face flashed red. "Oh, I get it, all right. Just wait till Mr. Robert E. Lee Yates gets home in a few days. I'm going to let him have it something fierce!"

"Naw, Mrs. Elizabeth—"

"Liz."

"Looka here, Mrs.—Liz, we gonna be friends, you

can't be tellin' on us like that. He'll know quick as anything it was us that told you. You'll get us in a peck of trouble—ever'body down here."

The houses were a stone's throw away now. The eight houses amid a small grove of pin oaks weren't as small as she had imagined, but they looked like a heavy thunderstorm would send them toppling to the ground. "I'm sorry, I won't say anything. I promise. Is that your house, Sadie?" Liz pointed to the big house at the intersection of two dirt paths.

"Yep, that's where we stay."

"You and your family and your parents?"

"My mama's dead—died deliverin' me. They wasn't nobody to help her 'cept the colored women down here in the quarters. They can deliver a healthy child just fine, but if they's problems, the baby ain't likely to make it and a lot of mamas don't, neither."

"Oh, Sadie, I'm so sorry."

"It's all right. Harriet's mama raised me like her own. I lived in they house till I got the job at the big house. Harriet had been workin' there a while, and she told Mrs. Yates about me. We been workin' for that lady nigh on fifteen years now—started when we was 'bout thirteen years old. When Harriet and them needed the room, I moved into Hiram's house. I call him Hiram 'cause Harriet's daddy was more like my daddy growin' up that he was. He a good man, and I always understood he was my daddy—that's just the way it was. He got the job takin' care of the sto' after my mama died, so he always been able to slip a little extra my way."

"Like what?"

"Sometimes a break when I was workin' the fields. He would come take my cotton sack and tell me to find me a hidin' place to take a quick nap sometimes. Sometimes a little money when I'd get a chance to go to town after I startin' workin' at the big house. Mrs. Yates made sure she found an excuse to take me or Harriet to town once every few months. She would buy us a little something on the side—a pretty dress for church or candy to share—so I never spent Hiram's money."

"Church?"

"Right there." Sadie pointed to several rows of logs sawn in half and propped with the flat sides up, set up in a semicircle under the largest of the oaks. "You ever sees a chance to sneak away on a Sunday morning and come down here, we'll show you black church. That's our only day off, so we got a reason to celebrate anyhow, but Hiram done always made church important to ever'body in the quarters. He do most of the preachin', and my brother lead the songs. We ain't got no songbooks. Wouldn't do no good 'cause most of these nig—most of these colored folks can't read nohow. So my brother sing a line, and then ever'body else sing it. All of Hiram's younguns can read, 'cause he taught us and we's teachin' our husbands and wives on Sunday afternoons when ever'body else is nappin'. Me and Mrs. Yates done taught Harriet good, too.

"One of these days, we gon' git up outta here and make somethin' of ourselves. No disrespect to you, Mrs.... sorry—Liz—but we got hopes and dreams bigger'n this place. Please, you gotta promise..."

"Stop right there. Robert is my husband, but please don't think I approve of the way…"

Harriet cut her off. "Looka here, don't go sayin' stuff about your husband you gon' have to deny later. Here's what you do, though: You go talk to Mr. Robert's mama real regular like. She'll let you talk open, and she'll tell you what you can do to help us if that's what you wanna do. But look, I hope you understand we didn't bring you out here today to git nothin' outta you. You been askin' 'bout where we live, and we thought it was best you see it for yourself rather than just hearin' 'bout it."

12

"Junior, I saw things that day that changed my perspective on how other people live. I saw the inside of the houses where Harriet and Sadie lived. I ate with them and the workers when they came in from the field. By the time I took my shoes off and walked barefoot back to the house that evening, I had become a different person. I determined to help those people living on our place as little more than slaves. The next morning, I sat down and talked to Robert's mother for several hours about giving them a chance at a better life.

"Besides everything else that happened on the day I visited the sharecroppers' measly dwellings, I was disheartened to see so many school-aged children coming in from the fields for lunch. Sadie told me the black schools shut down for cotton-picking season. Work in the fields took precedent over education. There were some poor white children working that day, too, and getting further behind in their learning. Mrs. Yates and I worked with Sadie and Harriet to not only teach them to read better but to train them to teach the others. I had gone to school through my tenth grade year, so I still had my old books that I used to teach them."

"Were they ever able to get off the farm, Grandma?"

"Sure did. That's an interesting story of God's providence, too. I'm going to be real honest with you about your grandfather, Junior. He spent a lot of time in town, drinking and carousing. I was young but not stupid. Being married didn't stop him from pursuing other women, but I'll leave it at that. The longer we stayed married, the longer he stayed away from home, except for a short period after your daddy was born. When Robert left home, I would always bake a cake and take it down to Hiram's store for him to give a little piece to everybody down in the quarters. He never told Robert.

"And Hiram—he was savvy, for sure. He figured Robert checked his books but didn't pay too much attention to the other tasks with which Robert trusted him. When Hiram talked him into painting our two barns, he ordered about twice as much paint as the job required. Hiram also convinced Robert that since everybody else's barns were red, he could save a good bit of money by painting them another color. When Hiram told him he found a good deal on green paint, Robert gave him the go ahead. The barns looked wonderful when the farmers finished painting them, as did every room on the inside of those houses! They cut the green with a few gallons of white Mrs. Yates picked up on the sly, and it made for a nice interior color."

"Really? How did y'all keep Grandpa from finding out?"

"I told you they painted everything on the *inside* of those houses. Robert would never even think of going inside the colored houses. He thought he might catch something if he did. It didn't hurt when Hiram told him a funny story every once in a while about a rat coming up through the hole of somebody's house in the middle of the night and causing a scare. They would laugh about it together, like Hiram was aligning with Robert against the colored folks. The rat story wasn't a complete lie, either, since it happened once. Because Robert wouldn't be caught dead in one of those houses, we fixed them up inside while leaving the outsides looking as dreadful as ever. He never discovered what Hiram did, either, as far as I could tell."

"So how did they leave?" Junior laid his full pan of peas next to the two grocery sacks full of hulls and leaned back in his chair.

"The Depression hit us all hard, but life started whaling away at Robert first. One day not too long before the stock market crashed, I walked over to visit with Mrs. Yates one morning like I did every day and found her dead in her bed. She had died in her sleep with a curious smile on her face. She had been feeling sickly for a while, and I think she realized she didn't have long. Anyway, she had told me that when she died, I should find her copy of *Pilgrim's Progress* on her bookshelf and lose no time getting it to Hiram.

"Robert had been in Jackson for a week and was supposed to return that afternoon. I found the book and hustled it down to Hiram before even telling anybody else Mrs. Yates had passed. When he opened it, he found an envelope inside where the middle part of the book should have been. He pulled out a letter and a pile of cash. The letter told him she appreciated everything he and his family had done for her through the years. She recognized Hiram had skimmed enough off of Robert to take his family and start a new life for himself somewhere else, but she wanted him to be able to buy some land of his own. She wanted everybody else in the quarters to have the same opportunity, so she crafted a plan for them. Hiram read me a part of the letter revealing just how wily my mother-in-law had been:

> Hiram, I love my son, but I won't say I like him. I especially don't like the way he treats people he sees as "below" him. If you need any of this money to help your family move far away from here, use it. Make sure you go a long way off because if Robert ever gets his hands around your neck, he would kill you. Use whatever you don't need to square the books with everybody in the quarters so nobody owes my son a dime. Record it in the books and get everybody out. Waste no time. Execute the plan.
>
> Give the rest of the money to Ben Laughlin, our neighbor to the east. He'll be expecting you. He treats his farmers right, pays them a fair price for their crops so they can have a decent living and maybe have some land of their own. He will wait for an appropriate time to buy a sizable piece of our property and hire the ones from our place who want

to stay in the area. Elizabeth will determine the right time.

"Robert's mother's death shook him up bad, in part because he didn't have to be out of town when she died. He was in Jackson carousing, knowing good and well her time was near. Her funeral was at the white church in town with burial at the cemetery on the other side of the railroad tracks. By the time his cousins had fed us back at the church fellowship hall, we were close to dark getting back to the farm. The house was dead quiet, which drove him up the wall. He had started drinking on our drive home, so one more glass of whiskey sent him to bed. When he woke up in the morning, he realized there wasn't a sharecropper or a maid or a store manager left on the place."

"They ran away during the night?"

"No, they anticipated when we would leave for the funeral. By the time we left for town, they had loaded their stuff on wagons and started moving up the little dusty road toward the house. Hiram's family was halfway to California before Robert ever realized they were missing. That was blow number two for your grandfather. Harvest season was on us, and he didn't have anybody to bring in the crops. He hired out what he was able, but he left thousands of dollars in the field. That was 1929. The stock market crashed in September.

"He was getting desperate, thinking he would be the one to lose the family place. I think that's the first time the responsibility for taking care of me and your daddy really settled in on him. He worried a lot, which made him less cantankerous. One night, he sat me down and gave me the bottom line—at least as he saw it. After the horrible harvest with all of his farmers bailing on him, we couldn't afford new ones. I asked him about the money his mother left him, but he told me he had used it to keep the bank off his back about his buildings in town. It was the perfect storm. He had used our farm as collateral for the all those buildings, any of which he could have sold off easily enough in normal times. The Great Depression was not normal times, though, and he projected tough times for quite a while.

"He determined he would sell the farm and all but one two-story building for what he could get in order to see us through the hard times. He planned for us to live in the little apartment upstairs on the building we would keep, and he would try some kind of business in the downstairs part. That was on a Wednesday. His meeting with the president of the bank was scheduled for Friday. I went out for a walk during your daddy's nap the next day—your grandfather stayed home to watch him since we didn't have any servants to do it anymore. I wanted to see Ben Laughlin and tell him it was time.

"Friday morning, Ben came by and offered a decent price for half the place. Robert laughed at him and muttered something about it being mighty convenient he would have the money it took to buy land during those times. He insinuated Ben had hired his farmers from under him since several of them ran to him looking for work after they left us. Ben didn't take kindly to that remark at all. He turned away, but Robert was smart enough to not let his only route to keeping part of the family homestead walk out the door. He accepted Ben's deal.

"As Robert signed the papers, he looked up at Ben Laughlin and told him if those 'darky traitors' knew what was good for them, they would watch their backs. Ben was even-tempered but not one to retreat from a threat. He moved so close to Robert that their noses almost touched. I acted like I wasn't paying attention for Robert's sake, but I heard Ben whisper, 'I know who you are and who you run around with in the middle of the night. If you so much as say a cross word to any of my people—white or colored—nobody'll ever find your body.'"

"Did he?"

"Did he what?"

"Ever say a cross word."

"Not that Ben Laughlin ever heard. Robert stayed bitter for the rest of his life, though, against all the ones who walked out on him and against Ben. He persuaded a few desperate sharecropping families to move in and help with what crops we could muster the next few years, but he had to do more of the work himself. The cotton market collapsed, so he shifted more to corn and beans, but we still barely made enough to get by most years. We constantly dipped into the rest of the land money to make ends meet. When the economy recovered after the war, Robert spent what we had left on farm equipment that let him farm more of the land and not depend on sharecroppers. They never stayed long anyway once they saw

Robert's true colors. He figured your daddy would help him like he helped his daddy."

"Grandma, who did Mr. Laughlin mean by the people Grandpa ran around with in the middle of the night?"

James Junior waited while his grandmother wiggled in the bed, trying to find a more comfortable position to rest her convalescing hip. "Junior, are you sure you want to hear this?" she finally asked.

"I want to know, Grandma. I already understand he was a mean man. I hope he never…"

"Say it."

"I hope he never hit you."

"No, he threatened a time or two, but I didn't stand for that. He was a coward at heart, although there were a few times I had to make myself scarce during his rants. But he inherited his daddy's hatred for colored people. One day, when Robert was off on one of his trips, I was cleaning so Harriet and Sadie could go help their families in the fields and spend time with them. I noticed some bed sheets folded in the top of his closet, so I pulled them down, only to discover a white robe and a white hood. Do you know what those mean?"

"Grandpa was in the Ku Klux Klan?"

She hung her head. "Yes, a leader, actually. I didn't know it until I found his robe and hood, but Ben Laughlin did. That's why he talked to Robert the way he did. I confronted Robert about it when he got home a few days later, and he told me to mind my business. I made it clear I was his wife, but I would not support any of that hatred. That's one of the times it crossed my mind that he might hit me, but I stood my ground, and he backed down. I have often wondered if I helped save somebody's life down the road by standing up to him. Even though he didn't quit the Klan, he understood I would give him up as quick as spit on him if he ever took part in the lynchings he was always threatening.

"When your daddy was five, he met a colored boy near the pond, right next to the part of the farm that was ours before Ben Laughlin bought it. Do you know your daddy's friend, Jeremiah?"

"Yes, ma'am."

"He was the colored boy. His mama and daddy were sharecroppers on our place who left and started farming on Ben's place. It was kind of funny they worked the same fields they always had, but they kept a little more, stayed in better houses, and paid fair prices at the store in town. Jeremiah was their youngest of a lot of children, and he just wandered off one day. Nobody noticed him missing, or they would have told him not to go near the property line. Anyway, he and Jimmy Lee had been friends for two years before Robert caught them at the pond together one day. Your daddy taught Jeremiah to read—he might have told you that.

"Anyway, Robert saw them fishing together one day and evermore let them have it. When Robert came back up to the house alone, I lit into him. I knew about Jimmy Lee and Jeremiah's friendship, and I did what I could to help them play without Robert's knowing about it. He was cussing and squawking about 'stringing up that nigger boy.' I told him he most certainly would not, and we shouted back and forth at one another. He ended up doing what he always did—drowning his frustrations in a whiskey bottle. I informed Ben Laughlin about our confrontation, and he made sure Robert still appreciated his promise from the day he bought part of the farm.

"Your granddaddy did his best to indoctrinate Jimmy Lee with that poison, but he was wise to the difference between right and wrong at an early age. I'm sure proud of the man your daddy's turned out to be. After what I've told you today, I hope you see what a turnaround he's made in our family tree in just one generation."

"Second biggest, maybe," James Junior said. "Grandma, can I tell you something?"

"Sure, anything, sweetie."

"I didn't really want to come stay with you this summer."

"Of course you didn't. What sixteen-year-old-boy in his right mind wants to give up a summer of swimming and fishing and running around with his friends to stay with his old broken down grandmother?"

"I'm glad I came, though. My attitude toward helping you from now in is going to improve—I promise. I love you, Grandma."

JAMES JUNIOR WALKED to his empty chair after he finished his story. When nobody in the room said a word, he stopped before his father and continued. "Pops, when I watched you and Jeremiah walk into church together after all those years, it was one of the proudest moments of my life. Long before then, you had taught me not to judge people by the color of their skin. But that day showed just how hard you had worked to change our family tree. I love you, Pops." James Junior leaned over and kissed his father on the cheek.

Laticia recovered first and asked, "All right, who's next?"

Nobody moved.

EASTON

13

Easton finally spoke up. "No way I can follow that, but I'll take the hit." He waited until James Junior had returned to his seat before walking to the front.

"I'll start with a quick summary of my history with this group for the new folks. This time last year," he began, "I was lamenting having a wasted day before my business meeting the day after Thanksgiving. I had already enjoyed another record sales year, but my appetite for the sale stayed insatiable, just like my appetite for the win did as an athlete. I might have been a first-round draft pick with a solid chance of being a big leaguer one day. While I was rehabbing from an injury during the summer before my last college season, I picked up a job with a medical company because of my name, honestly. I rode along on sales calls, signed a few autographs, which should have been the extent of it. But one day I made a sale—not a big one compared to the deals I put together these days—

but one that caused me to fall head over heels for a new scoreboard.

"I'm telling you the truth when I say money doesn't mean much to me, but it is a way to keep score with all the other salesmen in my company. I've been there six years now, and the only year I didn't come out on top was my first partial year with the company. This year has been different, though. I'll still finish on top by a wide margin, but that's based on the work I've put in to build all the relationships I have now.

"Last year, I had some time to kill before supper. I didn't realize it until I met with Lonesome, Party of Six, but I filled every moment of my time running from something. I never realized I needed to close the door on my baseball career but thought I could just move on. But baseball success was a dream, a big one that came crashing down when I blew out my arm. Perhaps the injury wouldn't have fazed my ability to get hitters out, but I was okay with never knowing. Anyway, by my choice or not, my dream died. Before supper last Thanksgiving, I stopped by the ballpark over at the college. That's where I injured my arm, and I had no idea how the memories would come flooding back.

"The front gate was unlocked, so I walked out toward the field. The gate at the field stood open, so I kept walking onto the field, half expecting to hear some old codger yell, 'Hey, you don't belong on the field!' I would have agreed with him, too. But nobody showed up, and I kept walking all the way to the mound. The game I pitched on that mound back in the day was the best game of my life. I remembered almost every pitch, so I went through the pitching motion again and again as if it was actual time. I recalled the smells of the grill, the look on their best hitter's face when I made him look silly on a slider in the dirt, the sounds of the local heckler—I carried on an internal conversation with him for most of the game. He tried to get in my head, but I owned him in there.

"When I made it to the bottom of the eighth of my mock game, I needed three strikeouts to break the conference record for strikeouts in a game. I remember every pitch, every location, every result being as real as it was so many seasons ago. On the pitch where my arm snapped, it was like I hurt it all over again. That's when I fell apart. I couldn't understand it until Pastor Hobbs here taught me about grieving a loss. After all you guys left last year, Pastor Hobbs and I stuck around for another cup of coffee, and I did something a million miles from my mind when I drove down to Harriston the day before: I gave my life to Jesus.

"You guys remember me talking about my assistant Sherrill last year…"

"Your assistant?" Paula Gull asked. "Wasn't she your —what was it you called her? She had some fancy title, right?"

"*Executive coordinator,* yeah. Most people outside of our business circle don't understand that term, so it's easier to say *assistant.*"

"You married her yet?" Paula asked.

"Don't start again." His cheeks flushed a little when he said it.

Paula shrugged. "Just saying."

"What I was going to say is Sherrill had pushed me to take my family—my brother and sister and their families—on a trip. I'm back here this year to report that Easton Sterling took a full week off from work last year. How 'bout them apples?"

Paula golf clapped along with the rest of Lonesome, Party of Six. "Still Mr. Important, though, huh?" He raised an eyebrow. "Speaking of yourself in the third person?"

"Oh, sorry. One of my pet peeves, too, and there I go doing it. Anyway, I had Sherrill rent this huge beach house right on the gulf in Destin, and we went down in June. We came through Harriston on the way down, and I enjoyed lunch with Pops while Ronnie and Grace found a place with a playground to their kids work out some of their pent up energy. I kind of needed a break, too, because Sherrill made me promise to ride with my family instead of driving. She knows it would have been too easy to check out and try to work if I drove my car. I switched vehicles every time we stopped, but I was ready for an intermission by the time we made it to Harriston, and they dropped me off to visit with Pops. Pops is a lot quieter than my nieces and nephews.

"So we arrived in Destin on a Saturday afternoon—Sherrill got the house through a client of ours, so we avoided the Sunday traffic and got to keep the house through two weekends. While we had visited in Harriston, Pops reminded me how I jumped full bore into baseball and then into sales, and he suggested I do the same with family vacationing. So I did. Every time I wanted to make a call or just check in with Sherrill, I remembered my job that week was to reconnect with my family, and I would leave the phone powered down. I checked it right before breakfast, lunch, and supper to see if Sherrill had texted, but she was as devoted to my vacation as I was. We have a few needy clients who can get straight through to me if they need anything, but I think Sherrill threatened them within three inches of their lives if they called me during my beach week. By Wednesday or Thursday, I wondered if the company had gone out of business and just forgotten to tell me, but I had promised Sherrill I wouldn't call unless it was an absolute emergency, and my curiosity didn't qualify.

"I stirred at least an hour before everybody else each morning to read and swim laps. My brother would bring me a cup of coffee by the pool, and my sister joined us by our second cup every day. I apologized a lot to both of them, but by the third day, they told me to stop groveling and move on. We had a solid hour together every morning before their kids started staggering downstairs. Ronnie's wife and Grace's husband took care of the kids in the morning so I could catch up with my siblings. We'd all play at the beach later in the mornings, come back to the house for lunch and naps—me included, most days—and we'd try a new seafood place every night. One night in particular, I had quite an unexpected encounter."

"Easton? Easton Sterling?"

It took Easton several scans of the place before he

recognized the well-tanned face to his left, a familiar face in an unfamiliar place.

"Barry Needham. What brings you here?" Easton asked, his reflexes reaching for the hand not yet extended toward him.

Needham took it, which surprised Easton later when he thought back on the encounter. "I'm spending the money you sent me. Never would have spent it this way before I got one-upped by a rising star."

Easton excused himself from his family and walked outside with Needham and his date. "Look, Barry, I handled this whole thing wrong."

"It's all good. I was getting a little too content at Mid-South when you pulled the carpet out from under me, anyway. Oh, I'll admit, I was sore at you for a good long while, and I certainly wasn't going to stay at the same company as you, but I had to let it go eventually, you know? You put a little fire back in my belly for a last hurrah over at Landrith Medical."

"You still over there?"

"Nope, called it a career three weeks ago. Been here ever since."

"You moved here?"

"No, but your check helped me put a down payment on a condo down here. Could be I'll be end up as one of those snowbirds, you know?"

"About that, Barry. I'm glad you're enjoying the money that should have been yours in the first place, but you deserve more than the commission. I have wanted to tell you I'm sorry for undercutting you and ask you to forgive me for doing that to you."

"Why didn't you?"

"I don't know. Scared, I guess."

"Scared—the great Easton Sterling? You going soft, Sterling?"

"No, just... making changes and dealing with some regrets."

"If you weren't a six-four pretty boy, I would've talked myself out of believing it was really you in there. That your wife in there—the brunette? She's a real looker."

"Watch it. She's my sister."

"Sorry. You married? Any of those your kids?"

"No wife, no kids."

"Lots of nieces and nephews, evidently."

"Yeah, they're a handful, but we're having a great time. Haven't quite caught up to your tan, though, Barry."

"You're different, Sterling." He opened his mouth to say more when the hostess announced, "Sterling, party of twelve."

"Good to see you, Easton," Needham said, reaching to shake his hand again. "Really, and thanks again for the check."

"So, are we good?" Easton asked, clasping the hand in front of him and holding it as he waited for the answer he needed to hear before joining his family.

"Yeah, we're good. Go live your new life."

"Thanks, Barry. Really. Thank you."

"MAKING things right with Barry was cool. I had been feeling God pushing me to do that, and so was Sherrill —sometimes it's hard to tell the difference between her and the Holy Spirit, to be honest. There's another conversation I wanted to tell you guys about that has led to something incredible and unexpected. I haven't even told Pops yet.

"I was sitting by the pool one morning, just me and Ronnie talking about some of our ball games back in the day. We played on the same high school team for one year. He was the captain, a senior catcher, and I was the hotshot freshman pitcher. Our coach did what coaches ought to do—gave all the older guys a chance to pitch before I got in a game. Once I did, though, everybody on the team understood I deserved to pitch. I'm not trying to be arrogant, I'm just saying. Ronnie and me took our natural chemistry as brothers right into our pitcher-catcher relationship, even though we had never played on the same team before. We had played catch in the backyard since I could pick up a ball, though, and he always threw tough situations at me and made me pitch out of them. When we took the field together at long last, I knew what pitch he was going to call and the location he wanted before he ever put the signal down between his knees.

"We had an unbelievable time together that year. I eventually became a starter in our district games, heady stuff for a freshman. When I took the field, though, I was back on that old dirt pile Ronnie and I built and called a mound in our backyard. He could have played college ball, but his knees started causing him some problems, and he decided he would never have as much fun playing ball as he had that year.

"Ronnie had just said he had something interesting to tell me when Doug—that Grace's husband—came down to join us. We asked where Grace was, and he said she heard us talking baseball and figured Doug would enjoy the conversation more than she would." Catching Grace's eyes at his table at The Log Cabin, Easton added, "Not that Grace couldn't hold her own on the ball field. She kind of had to if she wanted any kind of relationship with her brothers back then—she's between Ronnie and me in age. She was talented enough to play college softball, so I'd say she did okay." Grace smiled and motioned for him to share his news.

14

Doug grabbed a deck chair and asked, "What game are y'all reliving now?"

Ronnie said, "We just re-won the district championship with a freshman on the mound against a senior. Best game I ever caught. They had three hits, and two never left the infield." He snickered and added, "We read Easton's name in the paper the next morning, but a pitcher is only as good as his catcher."

"Right," Easton said, rocking back in his chair. "Guess I had a talented group of catchers through my entire career. Doug, you were a pitcher—you agree with my big brother's somewhat egocentric opinion?"

"Absolutely. He got me a two-hitter just last week." Ronnie smiled and lifted his coffee cup as a toast.

"Wait, what do you mean, last week?"

"You miss a lot, not being around anymore."

"Are y'all playing ball again? Where?"

Ronnie said, "Adult league in Memphis. My knees

can handle playing once or twice a week as long as we don't have any practices in between."

"And, Doug, you're pitching again?"

"First time I'd picked up a ball in at least five years, but it all came back pretty quickly. The league is mostly washed-up old college players. You should join us. We could use a rag arm lefty starter." Ronnie laughed and punched Easton in his tricep.

All three men sat in silence until Easton asked, "Do y'all really enjoy playing with a bunch of has-beens?"

Ronnie knew his younger brother was hooked. "We have a blast. Doug and I talked about it last year after we went to watch a buddy of ours play, and we gave it a go. The level of talent is not bad, like fall scrimmages in college. Most of the teams have several guys who were solid players five or ten years ago but never got the chance to play pro ball. Doug and me hold our own. Doug threw that two-hitter last week, maybe not against the best team in the league, but nobody at his office has to know that."

"Yeah, plus seven days later, I'm finally starting to feel Ol' Righty again," Doug said, rubbing his right arm. "She doesn't bounce back quite like she used to, but she can still snap off a curveball like back in the day. What do you think, Easton? Wanna toss the ol' horsehide?"

"Here? Now? Nah, I haven't thrown a ball since college. Plus, I wouldn't even be able to find my glove."

Ronnie stood up. "I'm going for a second cup. Anybody ready?" Easton handed him his mug and Doug declined.

When Ronnie disappeared into the house, Easton's

curiosity got the best of him. "Doug, you pitched in college, in front of raucous crowds and all."

"Nothing resembling the crowds you saw, but yeah."

"So what's it like pitching in a men's league? Does anybody come to the games?"

"Wives and girlfriends, mostly, and a few parents. Some of us have kids who get a kick out of watching their dads out there acting like kids themselves. Easton, I'm telling you, I insisted I was finished with this game when I threw my last game in our conference tournament my senior year. Not my best effort, but I was ready to turn the page. This, though, this is… fun. I'm not sure I noticed when the fun left the game. College, I guess. I mean, I had a blast playing college ball, but I think it was more about having fun with my teammates outside of baseball. I still enjoyed the games, but they were more businesslike than high school. I guess when your coaches' jobs are on the line based on how you play, it's not the same as playing for somebody's dad at twelve years old."

"I can see that. For me, it was always about competing, beating the other club, striking out the other batter, battling with my teammates and against them, too. It never satisfied me simply to be a part of the team. I wanted to be the most important player, too. Sales lured me like that, too, but I'm viewing life differently since I started following God. I just wish…" Ronnie burst through the kitchen door. "Hey, what's this? That doesn't even resemble a cup of coffee."

Ronnie tossed him a mitt with a baseball nestled

inside it. "Found it at Mom's house. It has been sitting there waiting for you since... since when?"

"State championship." Easton slipped the glove onto his right hand and just as naturally propped the baseball between his thumb and middle finger and snapped it skyward. In college he broke in a new glove every year, but this old one fit perfectly and held stories he would never forget.

"Still working on the ol' Uncle Charlie, I see," Ronnie said. "Doug, this kid used to walk around school, snapping a baseball in the halls, at lunch, in the classroom... until Ms. Bennett took it away from him one day."

Easton smiled as the memories that seemed so far in his past came flooding back. "She was there at the state championship. When she gave me a hug after the game, she pulled the ball from my glove and said, 'Now, how's that work again' and snapped it up in the air. Then, she reached into her purse and pulled out the ball she took up when I was in ninth grade. She used it to figure out how I flipped it like I did and figured if we won state, she would show off her new skill and give my ball back. She told me how proud she was of me. That meant about as much to me as striking out their cleanup hitter to win it."

"So, what do you say?" Doug asked, pounding his fist inside his own glove that Ronnie had retrieved along with Easton's and his own.

"Play catch with my state championship ball?"

"You'll find it's similar to any other ball. We'll swap it out if it means that much to you, though."

"Let's take it to the beach," Easton said, snapping it to Ronnie.

"HEY, kids, look, your Uncle Easton can still throw and catch a baseball!" Doug exclaimed.

"Daddy, why does Uncle Easton throw wronghandeded?" four-year-old Preston asked.

"Beats me. Uncle Easton, why do you throw wronghandeded?"

Easton laughed and walked over to Preston. "What Uncle Easton does is throw *left*handeded. If you pitch with this hand, the coach gives you more chances than if you're righthandeded like your daddy."

Preston huffed and crossed his arms over his tiny chest. "My daddy pitched last week. When was the last time you pitched, Uncle Easton?"

Easton wagged his finger toward Doug. "You told him to say that."

"Oh, yeah, because I'm that good. I can convince a four-year-old to say what I want on cue. Thanks for the compliment on my mad daddy skills."

Preston glared at his dad and declared, "I'm four-and-a-half" before spinning around and joining the other kids gathering under the multi-colored umbrellas Grace and Doug's wife, Samantha, had staked into the sand.

"Hey, Preston!" Easton yelled after his nephew, "You want to see Uncle Easton pitch? Here, watch this!" He motioned for Ronnie to drop into a catcher's stance. He wound and fired a fastball toward his brother. Ronnie didn't have to move his mitt as the pitch found its mark. The loud pop of Ronnie's mitt garnered looks from several bystanders.

POPS GRINNED at Easton's story. "You stepped back on the mound, didn't you?"

"I did. You know me well enough by now to recognize the competitive spirit that has driven me my whole life took over the first time I made Ronnie's mitt pop. When we got back home from the beach, I didn't even give Ronnie and Doug time to unpack. We met at the ballpark where they play, and I threw thirty or forty pitches, mostly fastballs. I tried the slider to see if she still worked like she used to."

As with many older sportswriters, James Junior never went anywhere without a little notebook tucked in his shirt pocket. He had it out now, sniffing a story. "So did she?" Easton's broad smile told him everything.

"I threw to Ronnie a couple more times, and he declared me ready. I showed up to the game to pitch against a team that had beaten Ronnie and them earlier in the year. They hadn't heard I was going to be playing for the Sting—that's the name of our club—before the game. When I struck out all three batters in the first inning, I listened as some of their players asked who this guy was. Some guys about my age started telling them stories about me while I was pitching. I was tracking with them because I have an uncanny ability to concentrate on several things at once while I'm on the mound. I can't explain why because I'm so singularly focused doing anything else.

"Anyway, the plan was for me to pitch three innings the first time out, but I ended up going five. A little bloop double was the only hit I gave up. Didn't walk anybody, either."

"Strikeouts?" James Junior asked, barely looking up from his already crowded page.

"Fourteen."

The reporter stopped jotting notes. "You had fourteen strikeouts in five innings?"

"Yeah, one guy tried to bunt for a hit. Ronnie threw him out by plenty. Next to last batter I faced flared one over the first baseman's head for their one hit. Good thing, too. If I still had a no-hitter, they couldn't have pried the ball from my hand."

"How many games did you end up throwing?"

"Five."

"What were your numbers?"

"Four wins, no losses, twenty-five innings, seven walks, fifty-three strikeouts."

"Earned run average?"

"Zero."

"You didn't give up any earned runs?"

"I didn't give up any runs at all."

"Wow, that's amazing. How old are you, Easton?"

"Twenty-seven. I'll be twenty-eight next month."

"Twenty-seven, huh? You know, they say…"

"Yeah, the age twenty-seven season is a player's prime. Sure felt like it this summer."

"Have you ever considered perhaps it's not too late to make a run at a big league career? It's not unprecedented, you know. I'm sure you watched the movie about the guy who made the Rays. He was a lot older than you are now."

"Junior, when I left baseball, I figured it was for good. But when I threw that first pitch to Ronnie on the beach, I had an inkling that my arm still had life. I never gave it much of a chance after rehab. I refused to waste time wondering what could have been.

"But there are several areas of my life I never 'wasted time' considering, things far more important than how I earn a paycheck, that I revisited this year. I spent time with my mom—she had a terrible stroke a few years ago from which she didn't fully recover. I had a lot of ground to make up with Ronnie and Grace and their families. They have been forgiving, so I have been able to enjoy spending time with them. I'll tell you my favorite part of the 'new Easton,' though, and that's pitching to my brother and then handing the ball to my brother-in-law to come in to pitch for me. So—long answer to your short question—I had a blast focusing on the real and current, but there was this nagging idea in the back of my mind: Could I still make it to the big leagues?"

"Did you... think about doing anything? You know, a tryout?"

"James, I would have called you crazy at the beginning of the summer, but..."

"Did you do it? Go to a tryout?"

"No, a tryout sort of came to me. Last game of the

season, the tournament championship. I pitched against the regular-season champions who hadn't lost a game. Their entire starting lineup played major college ball, and most of them weren't much past their college careers. I hadn't pitched against them yet, so I looked forward to testing myself against them. We're ten minutes away from first pitch. I've already finished throwing my warm-up pitches in the bullpen. My family is there, all my nieces and nephews. Grace even picked up Mom and brought her. Sherrill had come to a couple of games during the season, and she was there. She couldn't believe I was pitching again. I imagine she wanted to see if all the stories other salesmen had told her about my playing days were true.

"I'm all keyed up, ready to go. Well, that's when my brother comes up to me and says, 'Don't look now, but the Cardinals' assistant general manager is sitting three rows behind home plate.' I didn't believe him, but some important-looking guy was there all right, with a leather notebook and a radar gun. Something didn't seem normal because a general manager doesn't go to games like ours; scouts do, and they don't scout washed-up men's league games. Nevertheless, there he was.

"I didn't have time to process everything right before the game, so I called Sherrill over and asked her to snoop for me. She giggled at me and said she had never seen me so nervous. She had just walked away to make her way to the fourth or fifth row behind home plate when Ronnie strolled to the end of the dugout."

15

"Y ou ready, little brother?"

"I think so."

"Think so? When have you ever *thought so*? You aren't nervous, are you, kid?"

"Nah, just that guy…"

"You *are* nervous! Ha, first time for everything. All right, here's what we're going to do: This team believes they're going to knock you around and get themselves noticed by Mr. GM there, right? So we're going to pitch them backward. You almost always throw a fastball on the inside corner to start the game. Their first hitter is a lefty swinger. Tonight, we're going to start him off with a changeup inside."

"But you're never supposed to start off an at bat with a changeup, much less the first pitch of the game. And you're supposed to avoid low and in to a lefthanded batter. That's usually their sweet spot."

"Do you trust me, little brother?"

"With my life."

"Changeup low and in, slider away, fastball at the letters. Good morning, good afternoon, and good night."

Easton took the mound for his warmup tosses amidst less fanfare than he had ever experienced for a championship game. His youth travel teams had won several state championships, and his high school took three straight prep titles. His college team won the conference championship his junior year, his last, and might have gone further if he hadn't hurt his arm. Even without the roar of the crowd from previous title games, he sensed the adrenaline cursing down his arms and through his fingers. He motioned for Ronnie to throw down to second base and prepared to face the leadoff hitter for the Memphis Vipers.

Ronnie wiggled four fingers for the changeup. Easton nodded, wound, and fired. To the hitter, the pitch spun like the fastball he expected. When he began his swing, however, the ball seemed to fall off a table. The Viper batsman was so far out in front of the pitch that spun himself around and landed on one knee. He looked as helpless chasing a slider in the dirt for strike two and waving at a fastball at the letters to strike out. Easton winked at Ronnie as his Sting teammates tossed the ball around the infield after the strikeout.

After the inning, which included another strikeout and a weak pop fly, Easton found a spot near the back of the dugout as far from the field as he could sit. He didn't turn around when Sherrill approached the chain-link fence from behind. "What's the scoop, detective?"

"Oh, he's here to watch the former stud, all right."

"Did he say so?"

"Didn't have to."

"How do you know, then?"

"You just never stop selling me short, do you?"

"Okay, okay, my bad. What gives?"

"After you struck out the first batter, he jotted some notes and made a call. He read off some numbers. The numbers were how hard you were throwing, right?"

"Most likely. What did he say?"

"Eighty-two."

Easton's face fell. "Sure felt like more than that. Oh, well, it's fun being out there on the field with Ronnie, anyway. Thanks, Sherrill."

"That was just the first number. Don't you want the other numbers?"

"Wait, what?"

"Yeah, eighty-two was the first pitch. The others were *eighty-seven* and *ninety-four*. The higher the better, right, depending on what pitch you're throwing?"

Easton's face brightened. "Ninety-four! Sherrill I could kiss you right now!"

"Well, that would be weird."

"No, you don't understand. Hey, Ronnie, come here. Sherrill, tell him. Just the numbers. He'll understand what they mean." She repeated the numbers.

"Ho-ly cow," Ronnie mumbled. "What did you throw before?"

"Ninety-six, ninety-seven. Ronnie, I could throw that hard *tonight*."

"Don't you go throwing your arm out again, kid."

"No, listen. A pitcher never hits his top velocity in the first inning. Ronnie, I might throw harder than I ever did. Tonight."

"Not at the expense of your change-up and slider." Ronnie laughed. "That first batter cussed every step back to the dugout. Shoot, they haven't even seen your curve yet. I've always believed that was your most underrated pitch. Let's show it off to the first batter next inning."

The first batter for the Vipers in the second inning, a righthander, swung and missed at two fastballs. He watched a third pitch that started well outside before it veered right over the center of the plate for a called strike three. A weak grounder to the second baseman and another strikeout later, Sherrill was back for another report.

"Mr. Sterling, you might have a professional decision to make after the game tonight."

"Huh?"

"From what he's saying to whoever he's talking to on the phone, he might offer you a contract tonight."

"No way. That kind of stuff doesn't happen. They've got to run it through all sorts of channels before they…"

Ronnie was shaking his head fervently. "No, don't you see? Scouts have to pass it up the chain of command until it gets to the GM. Easton, he *is* the GM, at least his assistant. That's got to be his boss he's talking to about you."

"Still, what's he even doing here?"

"In town to watch the Redbirds play," Sherrill said. "Somebody tipped him off that you were pitching again.

The Redbirds—they're a St. Louis minor league team, right?"

"Yes. How do you know?"

"I'm close enough to overhear everything he's saying on the phone, even though he's keeping it as hushed as he can. The Redbirds played a day game today, and he was going to go back to St. Louis afterward, but he was curious about your pitching again. If you had anything remaining in the tank, he wanted to be the one to rediscover you. I'd say he's glad he came. He's talking to the other guy about how to get you to sign before anybody else finds out you're playing again."

"What makes him think I want to play again?"

"He probably assumes any former athlete wants to be one again. Why else would a successful professional salesman play in a league like this, right? I could convince him to move along, nothing to see here."

"No, don't, Sherrill. I sure didn't see this coming tonight. Give it another inning, okay?"

"He's bound to become suspicious if I keep coming to the dugout between innings. What if he asks questions?"

"You've been my front man… uh, person, for years. You'll figure out something. Tell him you're my girlfriend if you have to."

Sherrill contorted her mouth. "This game makes you say strange stuff, Sterling. I'm going to the concession stand now. This covert operation is making your amateur sleuth hungry."

The Sting plated a pair of runs in the inning to take

the lead. As they took the field for the top of the third inning, Easton put his arm around his catcher. "What's your plan for this inning, big brother?"

"Heaters. Lots of 'em. Big boy has seen enough of your off-speed stuff to realize you've still got it. Let's try to break that radar gun without breaking you."

Easton grinned and threw nothing but fastballs with his seven warm-up pitches. The first batter whiffed on two fastballs before slapping a single to right field. The next batter struck out on three fastballs on the outside corner. With one out, the tall lefthander pounded two fastballs inside before hitting the outside corner with a pitch that the hitter grounded to the Sting shortstop for an inning-ending double play. Nine batters, nine outs.

In the fourth inning, Easton faced the top of the Vipers' lineup again. He and Ronnie determined to showcase Easton's fastball again. Two pop-ups and a strikeout later, they sprinted with their teammates from the field. Sherrill strolled over for another conference.

"Better decide which career you want to chase," she started. "That last pitch was ninety-eight. Easton, he pulled out a contract and started filling in the blanks."

"How much are we talking?" Ronnie asked.

"He hasn't said. How much is a lot?"

"Hard to tell," Easton said. "Doesn't matter as much as his telling me I still have what it takes."

"That is so strange to me. I understand I've never watched you play baseball before this summer, but it's strange to see you less than one hundred percent confident in yourself about anything."

"This is the first time I've seen anything else but pure confidence in him, either," Ronne said.

"I know, I feel like such a..."

"Woman?" Sherrill offered, shaking her fist at him.

"I was going to say *wimp*," Easton countered.

"It's not like you need the money, right?" Ronnie said. "Come on, let's go throw another shutout inning. These might be the final three batters we face as brother teammates."

"Aw, man, you had to go there. I like your confidence, though. Let's shut 'em down and hand this lead off to Doug."

Easton pitched his last inning as if all of his options were on the line with every pitch. Ronnie called a masterful set of pitches to each batter. Curve, fastball, change-up to strike out the first batter. Slider, change-up, slider to the second. Fastball, slider, curve to the third. All strikes. All swings and misses.

Ronnie caught Easton's high five coming off the field and turned it into a hug. "An immaculate inning, that's what they call that! Nine pitches, three strikeouts—doesn't get any more dominant than that! Bro, you were dealing!"

"That was fun, big brother. If I never pitch another inning of baseball, that's a good one to finish with."

"Yeah, but that's not gonna happen, is it? I see that glimmer in your eye, little brother. Nobody stands in the way of that look, right, Sherrill?" he asked as she approached the dugout fence.

"Nope. Is that it? You finished?"

"Yep, Doug gets the last two innings. If he blows this

lead, he'll never be able to show his face at family dinner again."

"So, come on, give us the scoop—what happened?" asked James Junior.

"Doug shut 'em down, we won, 3-0, and hoisted the trophy in front of our smattering of fans."

"Come on, don't keep us waiting. Are you going to play baseball again?"

The private room at The Log Cabin was still as everyone awaited Easton's answer.

He let the moment of tension sit, soaking up the anticipation. "So, the Cardinals' assistant GM comes up to me after the game and introduces himself. I recalled his name and remembered talking to him on the phone my junior year when he was just an analyst in their scouting department, just a few basic questions. St. Louis was one of the teams that liked me before I got hurt, but their first pick was too far down in the draft to have a chance at me. Anyway, I told him it was nice to meet him, as if I was meeting a client. He said he hadn't heard I was pitching again until that afternoon. He asked if I had done any tryouts with other clubs.

"I laughed and told him about throwing for the first time in seven years at the beach with Ronnie and Doug earlier in the summer. He said it looked like I was having a blast out there and wondered if it might interest me to have that much fun in the Cardinals' organization. It was a slick segue, I must admit. I told him I had a wonderful career and that I was making some changes to allow me to make more out of my life. He wondered if I ever envisioned how my career might have looked. Again, good hook. I recognized where he was going, but I bit anyway.

"No, I told him, my success on the baseball field had come through my ability to stay focused on one thing and my sales career had taken off for the same reason. 'Not one time?' he asked. I didn't lie to him. I told him when I found out he was there to watch me pitch, I wondered if I still had what it took to get to the big leagues. He responded that the answer to my question was an unequivocal *yes*. He wasn't even through saying it when he pulled out a contract from his bag and said, 'Tell me what it would take."

"I told him any offer they made would be their chance to show how serious they were. He asked me to give him three days without talking to any other clubs. I told him I had no interest in pursuing anybody, that I was content where I was in life and couldn't promise I would even accept a serious offer. He asked again, and I promised him three days of silence.

"Well, news travels fast in the baseball world, and the Twins and Marlins reached out the next day. The day after that, the Orioles, Rangers, and Phillies called. True to my word, I didn't answer any of the calls or texts. Two nights after his assistant watched me pitch, the Cardinals' GM emailed me a contract. He said it had plenty of room for negotiation, which you just don't tell a guy you're trying to sign. His assistant convinced him to come hard with his first offer and be ready to increase it if needed. The contract was right up my alley—serious enough on the signing bonus but loaded with incentives. Make the big league club, get an extra $100,000. Make the club out of spring training the first year, double that. All those incentives added up to half a million besides a million-dollar signing bonus. That's an insane offer to somebody who's been out of baseball for seven years that you've seen pitch five innings. Teams take chances like that nowadays, though, and this guy remembered how driven I am, which is unusual for a number cruncher drowning in data. I legitimately had a decision to make."

"How long are you planning on stringing us along?" Pops asked. "I'm already ninety-three."

"All right, here goes. I did not play for the Cardinals' organization this summer. I signed to come to spring training and give it a go. Y'all understand who I am at my core—I expect to make the big league club sometime next year, and I'm working my rear end off to be ready. Sherrill is taking over my spot with Mid-South Med for the time being. My clients understand, and most of them are excited for me. They trust Sherrill, and she can do everything I would do for them, and then some. She'll knock down some serious money for a year or two, at least. If I can't cut it in The Show, I'll come back and never wonder if I had what it took again. So there you have it."

"What about the girl?" Paula yelled. "What about Sherrill?"

"She's doing great. You should have seen her face

when she got that first big check. She doesn't need any of it, but, boy, she sure loves giving it away."

"Geez, Mr. Important, you say more words to say nothing at all than anybody I've ever met."

"What do you mean?"

"Did you ever ask her out?"

Easton grinned, tickled at getting under Paula's skin. "I saw where you were aiming. I remember how insistent you were last year that somebody you had just met and somebody you hadn't even met were so meant for each other. Well, it turns out maybe we weren't."

"You never asked her out, did you?"

Easton looked back to his table, where Grace looked up from her phone and shrugged. "You might as well tell her. She sounds as persistent as you are."

Paula rubbed her palms together. "Give us the goods."

"Okay, after I got the contract offer, I took a few days to mull it over. I talked to Ronnie and Grace first. Neither of them thought I should have walked away from baseball in the first place, so they were all about my giving it a shot. I talked to the general manager of my company's branch next. He wasn't as excited about my opportunity as Ronnie and Grace were. However, he was on board with my plan to transition Sherrill into my role since she gave him his best opportunity to keep posting the best sales numbers of any branch in the company.

"All I had left was telling Sherrill. Now, I will admit since you pressed me so hard last year about her, I wondered if maybe I was missing something. I mean, we have a fantastic working relationship, and now we're both excited about our faith and the good we can do in the world. Since we were moving the same direction in so many things, I decided to take a risk. First, though, I needed to talk to her about the possibility of her taking over my spot in the company. I figured, hey, I'll take her to dinner to talk it over under the guise of a business dinner and see how it felt.

"Sherrill knew I was about to make a decision that would affect her future, so she was anxious the week after the game. Toward the end of the week, I told her I was coming to some conclusions and wanted to let her in on my thought process. I asked her—real casual-like —if she wanted to go to this nice restaurant downtown to talk about it. It's not a super romantic place—that would have weirded her out like telling her I could kiss her at the ball game, even though that was a figure of speech."

"Mm hm," Paula grunted.

"No, seriously. Anyway, the peculiar look she gave me set me on my heels. I came up with something about celebrating the roll-out that week of the new software I had been working on, along with where I was on my baseball decision. She bought it, I guess, and we met downtown around six o'clock that Friday night. We had to wait for a table, so I attempted small talk. Not my forté."

16

"You talk to your folks this week?"

"My parents? Y-yeah."

"They doing okay?"

"Easton, why are you asking about my parents?"

"I'm trying to talk about something other than work. Guess I'm still not very good at it. I suppose I could ask you about church, but I was there on Sunday, too. Didn't figure you'd want to chat about baseball."

"How long have we been working together? I've seen you nervous more this week than in all the years I have worked for you combined."

"*With* me."

"Whatever. You're scared to take this step, aren't you?"

You got that right... wait, what step is she talking about? Time to come clean.

"Sherrill, the truth is..."

"Sterling, party of two. Sterling, party of two," the

hostess announced into the microphone. On one hand, Easton was relieved, but the break in the conversation forced him to work up to declaring his intentions again. Their table in the corner helped—he wouldn't feel like he was on a public stage. When he picked up his napkin to drop in his lap, he wiped his sweaty palms first. He wondered if Sherrill did.

"Okay, Sterling, spill it. Record-setting salesman or big league ballplayer?" Leave it to Sherrill to cut right to the chase.

"Record-*shattering* salesman," he corrected.

"Whatever. Give me the goods. You're already cutting into my weekend."

Ouch. Not exactly the response to a Friday night dinner I was hoping for. "Okay, we'll get it out in the open before we even order."

"Really, Easton, what's with you tonight? You act like you're on a first… Wait, are you…?"

She had given him an open door, but he didn't force himself through it. "I'm going to sign with the Cardinals," he blurted.

Sherrill fell against the back of her chair. "I knew it." Her face said stunned; her voice, resigned to his choice. "When?"

"Well, even though I've been pitching for a few weeks, I'm in no condition to pitch in professional ball. They would love to drop me into one of their lower affiliates just to get me a handful of innings this summer. By the time I was in pitching shape, though, most leagues at that level would be finished with their seasons. I may fly down to Mexico or the Dominican Republic to throw a few innings of winter ball, but we're looking at spring training in February as a real go date."

"What about your job? More to the point, how does your decision affect me?"

"I have spent a lot of time considering that. I met with Gerald earlier this week and told him I was taking the deal with the Cardinals. He and I…"

"You told him before you told me?" Sherrill looked genuinely hurt.

"No, Sherrill, don't…"

"You just told me you told him earlier this week. Easton…"

"Please, Sherrill, hear me out."

She sat back, exasperated but silent. She made a curt motion for him to continue. This was a hint of the old Sherrill, and Easton didn't like it.

"Look, it wasn't a cut against you that I didn't tell you first. Before I took this position, I realized I had once chance to shoot for the moon. I told Tom Silverman when he offered me this job that one of my conditions was that I got to pick my assistant. You were the only person I considered. I had more in mind for the job than a secretary, and hey—you've taken this whole *executive coordinator* title and run with it. I couldn't have done everything—broken all the company sales records and all—without you. There's no way I would have had time to help develop those pieces of software if you weren't running my accounts for me. I don't even consider them *my* accomplishments, but *ours*."

Their server arrived to take their order, shrimp and scallion linguini for Sherrill and grilled salmon for

Easton. She hadn't taken three steps toward the kitchen when Sherrill said, "On with it."

"Am I keeping you from something? Do you have a date later tonight?"

"Hardly. Quit stalling."

"Okay, here goes. I had to talk to Gerald first because he had to sign off on my idea. My plan, should you accept it, is to turn over all my accounts to you. You practically run them anyway. You choose your travel days, and you pick your assistant… or *executive coordinator*, if you go that route. Gerald has full confidence in your ability to do the sales portion of my position. Heck, he knows how much of it you do already. You wouldn't handle any of the software stuff, just the medical devices. Here's the catch…"

Sherrill giggled.

"What?"

"The *catch*?"

"Ha ha. The potential snag, then. You will get full commissions on sales while I'm off earning my bonus. If baseball doesn't work out, Gerald wants me back, even if it's a few years down the road. If all that happens, he would give you the choice of returning to the way things are now or sliding into your own sales territory. He mentioned dividing our current territory if either or both of us decide we don't want to be as aggressive. Anyway, we would spend the rest of this calendar year transitioning. It all depends on you. You would start earning commissions on the sales right away."

Sherrill feigned composure, but Easton caught her dabbing the corner of her left eye after he revealed his vision. "Easton, I may have underestimated you, and I didn't figure that was possible anymore. I was just messing with you about telling Gerald before you told me, but that's quite a plan. Quite an unselfish plan. I can't imagine making the money you've been earning. I mean, I'm already demolishing what my level of education says I should be making. You've been generous to me, and..." At this, Sherrill broke, and the tears came past her best efforts to block them. "If I might voice a few concerns..." she said, desperate to move back to even ground.

"Concerns? If you're concerned about doing this job as a woman..."

"No, not that. You know I don't lack for confidence."

"You're worried about the tension between the job and your moral values?"

"No, actually, that's the biggest takeaway I've had over the last few months of watching you do it. I figured we would lose business after we gave our lives to the Lord, and you were so ready to share your changes with our clients. But you—*we* have built such good relationships with them that your honesty with them has made them more loyal to you. To us. I didn't think it possible."

"They see the changes in you, too."

"Tell me about it. Several clients have asked what's going on with us. Want to hear something funny?"

"No," he deadpanned.

"I'm going to tell you, anyway. Dr. Levitz from County General called about something a few weeks ago and asked if the rumor was true."

"What rumor?"

"That we had gotten married."

"Ha! What did you tell him?"

"What do you mean, what did I tell him? I asked where he got a crazy notion like that."

"What did he say?" Easton asked.

"He couldn't remember who told him, but someone had. I imagine somebody noticed the changes in both of us and made an assumption based on that. Who knows?"

Easton held his palms wide and shrugged. "I don't guess it's as farfetched as all that, when you look at it from the outside."

"What do you mean?"

He let the question sit for a moment before switching gears without further comment. "You said you had concerns. Like what?"

Sherrill giggled again. "Like who's going to buy your clothes and set up your family vacations and tell you where to go."

Easton smiled at the relaxed turn in their banter. "No problems there. I'll wear a uniform in my next job and have a clubhouse attendant wash it and hang it in my locker. He'll even pack my bags for me on road trips, so I won't forget anything important. Family vacations will be at the ballpark. I'll get the tickets, and Grace will take charge of everything else. As far as telling me where to go, the fans in our opponents' ballparks will take care of that."

"If you don't pitch well, your team's fans might join in."

"That's true. So, you're good with the plan? If you

need to talk through the particulars, maybe we can meet for coffee before work one day next week to consider your questions or legitimate concerns."

"Two chances in one week for people to see us in public together? Wow, you can't wait to get out the door, can you?"

Easton broke in, "No, don't take it…"

"I'm just kidding. Geez, Easton, you're acting like a middle schooler trying to talk to a girl for the first time."

"I just meant… I just want you to…"

"I DON'T REMEMBER EVER BEING SO flabbergasted in my life. I looked across the table at Sherrill laughing at me and considered the changes both of us had made since giving our lives to Jesus. When she stopped joking around, she folded her hands and leaned forward to rest her chin on them. The big smile she still had on her face practically glowed, and I realized I was staring at the most beautiful woman I had ever seen."

"Aw," Paula Gull said. "I knew you had it in you."

Easton shook his head. "I couldn't do it, though. The moment was so perfect that I couldn't—or at least, I didn't—risk messing it up."

Paula threw her hands in the air. "You've got to be kidding me. You—Mr. Singular Focus—didn't force yourself to stay on task long enough to see it through?"

Easton's memory wandered back to a corner table when his future seemed… right. "Oh, I was on task. For a reason I still can't quite explain, I couldn't make myself ask her on an actual date. The next day, Grace and I went out to breakfast, and I spilled everything. I'll give her credit— she didn't judge, just listened. I can't say my mind was any more clear afterward, but at least I had told somebody."

"You should have asked her out. She would have said yes."

Easton's eyes had been scanning the room as he spoke, making eye contact with everyone, as was his habit. He didn't identify who said it, but it was a familiar female voice.

"Who said that?" His gaze darted to his sister, who was looking at her phone and half paying attention. She glanced up and shook her head. "Not me."

Paula Gull's table claimed innocence.

"She would still go."

He recognized the voice as coming from his sister's area. He ruled out Laticia. "Austen?"

"Not me."

Everyone sat in silence for fifteen seconds. Finally, Easton said, "I don't guess it matters. Where was I?"

"Getting ready to ask me out, I hope," came the voice again. This time, Grace held up the face on her phone toward her brother.

"Sherrill? You've been listening to me ramble on about...?"

"Every word. Well said, boss."

"Stop it. Grace, you had some nerve... What if she..."

"There he goes again, speaking in half sentences,"

Sherrill said. "Isn't it fun to see him nervous over something, friend?"

Flustered, Easton's eyes darted back and forth between his sister and her phone. "Friend?"

"Ballpark buddies first. Easton, I had lunch with Grace after our... *moment,* as you called it. I usually guess what you're thinking before you've fully developed your ideas, but that was different—weird. She listened to me like she did you, and she stepped up to play matchmaker since neither of us was very good at the dating thing, apparently."

Paula stood and walked to Easton's side, hands on her hips. "Still *aren't* very good at it. Y'all are going to talk this to death, so I'm here to intervene. Hi, Sherrill, I'm Paula." Paula motioned for the others to join her, and they crowded around Easton and Grace.

"Hi, Paula. Easton has told me about you... all of you. Hi, everybody."

"Okay, now that we've finished the introductions—Easton, do you have something you'd like to ask Sherrill?"

Easton straightened to his full six feet four inches, took a deep breath, and asked, "Sherrill, would you like to...?"

"Easton, I... hold on, poor connection, I'm moving. Can you hear me now?"

"A little fuzzy, but go ahead."

"Easton, I..." This time the connection was gone.

"No, no, no! Call her back!" he demanded Grace.

"You call her back." She handed him the phone.

"Put in your passcode. Ugh, why is this so difficult?"

"It doesn't need to be."

That voice again. He spun around. "Sherrill."

"That's my name." She extended both hands to him. "I believe you wanted to ask me something."

He grabbed her hands before she had any chance to slip away again. "Sherrill, would you go on a date with me?"

She smiled like she had at the restaurant months before. "Yes, Mr. Sterling, I would love to go on a date with you. I thought you'd never ask."

"*I* thought I'd never ask."

"*We* thought you'd never ask," Paula said.

Holding Sherrill's hands in front of thirty other people, Easton said, "You came all this way."

Sherrill nodded. "I figure I knew most of them through you already. If we're going to start down this road, I didn't want to wait a year to meet your other family." Her vision for their relationship wasn't lost on Easton as he introduced her in person to his Lonesome, Party of Six family.

Laticia slipped out after a brief chat with Sherrill and returned with trays of sweet potato, pumpkin, pecan, and apple pies. She cut them into slices while Sherrill visited with Pops. She announced that everyone could make their way to the dessert table for some pie. "Two for you, Mr. Important, Mr. Singular Focus?" she asked Easton.

"Yes, ma'am. One day off from my training regimen for Log House pie like my mama's. And that's Mr. I've Got a Date to you, sister."

"Not if you don't get her away from Pops, you

don't." She pointed to Sherrill's arm wrapped around Pops' waist. Her head rested against his shoulder.

He walked over and pulled her two steps away. "Come on, Pops, you need to give me a head start."

Sherrill walked back over and snuggled up to Pops again. "Good thing I didn't meet him before you asked me out. He's got game. Maybe you should take lessons from him."

Easton threw his head back and laughed. "There's no doubt about that. Mr. Jimmy Lee, I'm going to need you to take care of her when she comes here to visit with our clients at the hospital while I'm at spring training."

"Oh, I'll be happy to look after her, Easton. She's a lot easier on these old eyes than old Ethel next door."

Easton's vision for their relationship was not lost on Sherrill. "I don't know how many of y'all have already told your stories this year, but I want her to share." She pointed to Paula Gull.

Easton smiled. "My nemesis, you mean."

"How's that?"

"She gave me a hard time last year about being so singularly focused that I hadn't even been out on a date in years. She was the one who first asked me why I hadn't taken you out."

Sherrill turned her brown eyes toward Easton. "And what did you tell her?"

Easton curled his right index finger and stuck it in his open mouth. Sherrill grinned and slapped his arm. "Was I that sickening to you?"

"I just never thought about you that way until Paula picked at me about you last year. We should thank her, though. It was her teasing that made me realize how much your countenance had changed since you started following God."

"And then I turned into the most beautiful woman you've ever seen?"

He blushed but reached for her hand. "Yeah, something like that."

She took his hand and stared up into his pale green eyes. "Mr. Sterling, when our kids ask about our first date, can we tell them this was it?"

He didn't flinch. "Tonight it is, Miss Riggs." They returned to their seats, both thinking *Sherrill Sterling* had a nice ring to it.

PAULA

17

"I don't know why I have to stand up here and talk," Paula Gull began, nodding at Easton and Sherrill, who couldn't take their eyes off each other. "My work here is finished. Seriously, though, I'm glad to have this opportunity to update all of you on everything that has happened in my life since last year. It wouldn't have been this amazing without you. Last Thanksgiving was one of the loneliest days of my life until I landed at the Lonesome, Party of Six table, but this past year had been the best.

"Austen, your generous act last year was simple, but so few people ever do something so selfless. I say that to thank you again for your thoughtfulness and to say it set the stage for me to evaluate my life to that point. Last year, my thoughts were so self-focused that I couldn't see the joy that should have been right in front of me. Instead of considering how happy Lisa was and how happy I should have been with her meeting Jake's parents and moving toward an engagement, I figured my lonely Thanksgiving would be the first of many more after she marries him and leaves me. Instead of thinking of David over in Iraq finishing out his last few months in the Army and how homesick he must be, I focused on my loneliness. Instead of being proud of the fine young man he is, I lived in fear of his becoming like his father."

One by one, Paula locked eyes with each of last year's party. "And then I met all of you. You encouraged me in the only role I ever embraced: single mom. You saw in my description of my children who they really were with my fears pulled aside. Thank you for that. But you also challenged me to consider who I am apart from them again. That's a neat trick, to get me to reflect on myself but not be self-focused. I'm still scratching my head about that part.

"It all started with welcoming Lisa home after her trip to Florida with Jake. She was so excited about meeting his family. With David already gone—at least for the next few months—I would have felt the pangs of loneliness thinking about her leaving. But I didn't." She took a sip of water and continued.

"Lisa wanted me to go to Florida with her to meet Jake's folks. Jake did, too, and they pressed me to take a beach vacation during spring break. I was reluctant. Like I told you guys last year, I've always wanted to go to the beach—been promised a beach vacation, even—but doing it at this stage in my life scared me. That probably sounds foreign to you, but my nose has been so close to the grindstone for so long that I only see what's right in front of me. But this was important to Lisa and Jake. Plus, I wanted to meet his parents before their wedding, for crying out loud.

"After a week, I softened a bit about going to the beach, and Lisa started looking at condos. She said Jake's folks would drive up and meet us and spend two or three days, but we would have the rest of the time to rest and relax. I deserved a break, she kept saying. When she showed me prices for a week in Destin, though, my heart rate shot through the roof. I'm sorry, y'all, I had no idea how much a week's vacation in Florida cost. Lisa patted my hand, said she understood, and left me alone. My mind scrambled to figure out a way to put together that kind of cash, plus eating out and gas and all.

"I wanted to make the trip happen for my girl, but I couldn't come up with a plan. I was disheartened, to say the least. Later, when I was brushing my teeth before I turned in for the night, my phone buzzed on the night-stand next to my bed. David was Facetiming me. This was one time I didn't feel like talking to him, but I answered anyway."

PAULA TOOK a deep breath and touched the green circle on her phone. "Hey, good looking."

"Hey, Mom. What's wrong?"

"Nothing. I'm just glad to see your handsome face."

"Come on, Mom. You realize I'm going to get it out of you eventually, so you might as well tell me."

Paula brought him up to date on her surprise Thanksgiving meal and her new friends. She told him about Lisa's trip and that she figured it was a matter of time before Jake popped the question. She described Lisa's excitement about her idea for a spring break trip to the beach to meet Jake's parents.

"And you don't want to go?"

"More than anything in life."

"Mom, everything you've told me sounds like fantastic news. What gives?"

The tears Paula had been trying to hold back burst forth with no restraint. David let her cry herself back into a semblance of control before she told him.

"So, Mom, it's just the money you're worried about?"

"Son, there has never been a moment of 'it's just the money' since I was sixteen. My top priority has been making enough to take care of myself and then you and Lisa after you were born. We've always made it, and I'm grateful for that, but when Lisa started showing me how much it costs to rent a condo in Destin—I'm sorry, I am overwhelmed right now."

"So it's just the money—nothing else?"

"No, what else would there be?"

"Uh, the notion of Lisa's leaving home?"

"I promise I'm okay with that. The time is right for my baby girl to fly the coop."

"Then it's just the money?"

"You keep saying that."

"Yes, Mom, because if it's the money, take everything you need for a dream vacation out of my account and go."

"David, I couldn't do that. It would take me months to pay you back."

"Then don't consider it a loan, Mom. It's a gift. I've been wanting to send you to the beach since you told me how my dad promised you a beach trip and never took you."

"But, Lisa and Jake…"

"Whatever is costs."

"But, David, that is your money."

"Mom, I joined the army with over ten grand in the bank, and my guys have been adding to it since I left. I don't drink or smoke, so I have very little to spend my army paycheck on, so there's plenty. Take the money."

"But what about college?"

"That's one reason I joined the army, remember, so Uncle Sam could pay for college."

"Oh."

"Mom, I'm not taking no for an answer. I'm not just okay with it, I insist. Promise to Facetime me from the beach, though. We have plenty of sand over here, but I want to see you digging your toes into a more relaxing kind."

"So you went to the beach?" Pastor Hobbs asked. "I remember from last year we had a common love for the beach."

Paula beamed. "I did. I hear people talk about their bucket lists of things they want to do before they die. My bucket list had one item: go to the beach."

"So, tell us about your trip."

"It was beyond anything I had ever dreamed. I remember every detail, but I'll skip to the highlights. David insisted—in*sisted*—that we not pick the bare minimum condo and eat fast food every night. He and Lisa picked the place. I didn't want to know how much it cost, but I admit I sneaked a peek after they booked it, and it's a good thing they booked it instead of me. In a million years, I wouldn't have paid that much for a house for seven days. Did y'all hear that? They booked us a *house*, for crying out loud, with enough bedrooms for Jake's parents to stay with us if they wanted. And they did.

"David also insisted on paying for a rental car for the week, too, and it was so nice! I can't even tell you the last time I got behind the wheel of a practically brand new car. I argued against it every step of the way, so David and Lisa Facetimed several times a week and set the plan in motion. Lisa wasn't as reluctant as me to spend David's money."

"Mom!" Lisa objected.

"Sorry, honey. I overheard Lisa and David's conversations some nights, and it was satisfying for me to hear my kids getting along and laughing and sounding like the grownups they had become at the same time. Not that they haven't always been close, but their having such a good time planning a beach trip for me was icing on the cake.

"So we arrived and found our beach house, which was as amazing in person as it was in the online photos. We walked out the back door and down a little wooden walkway and stepped off into sand. I kept walking right into the water. I stood at the edge for what seemed like an hour, feeling the waves roll over my feet and the sand squish between my toes. It was surreal. Lisa and Jake stood on our second story deck staring at me... and each other.

"I Facetimed David from the edge of the water after I sort of came back to myself. He was so happy he called several guys from his barracks over and showed me to them. He called that moment money well spent. I called it the dream of a lifetime. We arrived on a Sunday, and Jake's parents were set to arrive on Thursday, so we settled into a routine before they came. We walked to the beach after breakfast and coffee in the morning, stayed until lunch back at the house, and trekked back to the beach for a few hours in the afternoon. I encouraged Lisa and Jake to go do some things on their own, but they hung with me. We dressed up with our new tans at night and ate at some cool restaurants, thanks again to my wonderful son.

"The week was flying by way too fast when Jake's parents arrived on Thursday evening. Jeff and Sandra are outstanding folks, and we hit it off right away. We stayed up talking until one o'clock, but everybody woke up and prepared to go to the beach at our normal time.

Lisa told me they didn't want me to miss a minute. We took a break that afternoon, though. Lisa and I stayed at the house, ate sandwiches, and took a nap while Jake and his parents went out to eat and played a round of golf. Or so we thought.

"David picked out a super fancy restaurant for us for Friday evening. He said Saturday night, we would be too concerned with packing up and sad about leaving, so he wanted to send us a night earlier. You know, with the internet, you can plan a special beach trip from the other side of the world. We all dressed up and ate at an incredible restaurant. David made me promise one thing, that we would Facetime him from the beach when we returned from dinner. Our reservation was early enough to be back for the sunset, which was around four o'clock in the morning for David. He assured me that wouldn't be a problem for an army man."

———

DAVID WAS ready to Facetime his mother at 3:45 Iraq time. He stepped outside his barracks for a little privacy and dialed the number.

"Hey, honey."

"Hey, Mom. Are y'all back at the beach house?"

"Yep, on the walkway out front. I was reaching for my phone to Facetime you. The restaurant was unbelievable. Thank you so, so much."

"Mom, you don't have to keep thanking me for

everything. Hey, hand Lisa the phone. I want to see how you look. Wait, show me her first."

"Hey, little brother," Lisa said, posing for him.

"You're looking good, sis! All of you cleaned up well. I'm glad y'all had a blast. Hey, Jake." Jake waved behind Lisa. "All right, Lisa, grab the phone and show me my beautiful mom."

Lisa took the phone and stepped back from Paula. "Aw, Mom, you look stunning. I don't believe I've ever seen you dressed up like that before. I sure wish I was in Florida with y'all."

"Oh, David, I have wished that a hundred times since we arrived. Hey, I want you to meet Jake's parents, Jeff and Sandra." David waved at his phone, and they waved back.

"Nice to meet you," David said. "You ready?"

"We're ready."

"Okay, give the phone back to Mom." When Paula's wrinkled brow filled his screen, David said, "Mom, I'm going to need you to turn the phone around so I can see Jake, okay. Don't ask, just show me Jake, please."

Paula hesitated but turned her phone toward Jake. "That good?"

"Yep. Go, bro."

As Paula and Lisa tried to figure out what David was up to, Jake dropped to a knee and pulled a ring from his jacket pocket. "Because our families have shaped who we are, I wanted them to be here with us for this special moment. Lisa Gull, will you marry me?"

Lisa covered her face with both hands at first and bobbed her head up and down. As soon as she said yes, she spun around to look at her brother. "David, you knew?"

"In on it before Jake ever put a spring break trip in your mind. The tall task was talking Mom into going, so covering Jake's ulterior motive was easy. The surprise on your face made it all worthwhile. Congratulations, you two."

18

"What a splendid story—I love weddings!" Carol squealed. Looking around her tables filled with children, daughters-in-law, and boyfriends, she added. "Lisa, Jake's family will treasure you like I do my daughters-in-law. You'll be a beautiful bride, too."

Lisa stood and fairly sprinted to Carol's table. "Want to see my ring?"

"You bet I do, sweetie," Carol said, reaching for Lisa's hand. "When's the date?"

"December the fifteenth. We graduate in the morning and get married in the afternoon."

"Are y'all out of your mind, girl?"

"No ma'am. We're doing a small, private ceremony. The church where we're getting married has a little outdoor chapel, and it's just going to be us and our families."

"With David in person this time?"

"Yes, ma'am. We're so glad he's home."

"Well, honey, I hope your wedding is as memorable as possible. Better yet, I pray your *marriage* is as wonderful as Irv's and mine has been."

"Thank you, Ms. Carol." Turning back to the front, Lisa said, "Sorry, Mom, I didn't mean to break up your talk."

"It's okay, sweetheart. I can wait as long as you want to show off your ring. I need to tell one more story to my friends here, though. And to you and David."

Lisa returned to her table, reaching for Jake's hand. He took it and kissed her on the cheek. She stretched her other hand toward her brother. He took it and mimicked Jake, kissing her on the other cheek.

"So there it is," Paula said as the chatter settled down, "I finally got my beach trip, and my kids upstaged me." She laughed along with the rest of the room and continued, "And I wouldn't trade it for the world. There was another moment a few months later I wouldn't trade for the world, either. My son came home from the army safe and sound and even a few hours early."

Pops stood up and motioned for attention. "David, I'm certain I speak for all of us when I say thank you for your service to our country." He clapped and as the rest of the gathering rose and joined him for an ovation.

Paula beamed as she waited for the applause to die down. "David, I'm so proud of you my heart is about to burst wide open. Like I said earlier, when I came here last year, I was in the middle of a big pity party. Poor ol' lonesome Paula. She's gone and spent all this time doing everything for her kids, and now they've up and left her. Poor Paula.

"I'm not like most people. I guess I've known that my entire life. After we left last Thanksgiving, I spent the rest of the weekend pondering that some of you were dealing with much tougher situations than I was facing. Tara, you struggled to survive the night sober, only to face the same battle the next day. Carol, your husband was in the hospital. Pastor Hobbs, your wife had been murdered, and we were here on the day that meant the most to her. Pops and Easton and me were feeling sorry for ourselves. Sorry, guys, don't mean to pull y'all under the bus with me, but it's true.

"Easton, I believe the reason I felt comfortable messing with you last year was that I saw me in you. Similar to how you were so locked in on baseball and sales after that, I focused on my kids and surviving from one day to the next. I built a decent life for them and couldn't make myself look up long enough to realize it. When Pastor Hobbs said what you were experiencing was grief over a lost dream, it sounded silly to me at first. Later on, after I got back to the quiet of my apartment and replayed everybody's story in my head, it dawned on me that I had something I had never grieved over, either: my marriage. It some ways, that seems like another lifetime, but I had let a lot of resentment build up toward Brandon. I let my perspective of what happened make me fearful for what David would become. You guys helped me to realize that what my kids had already become was more important than my fears of what might, maybe, possibly happen to them.

"Anyway, Easton, I sat there and reflected on how you moved from one dream to another without thinking twice about it, like I did. You chose it and I didn't, but still, it caught up to you. Even though it has taken longer for me, it makes sense that my grief would catch up to me eventually, too. I drove to that little house where I raised my kids until Lisa started college. It was the house I ran away from home to, the house I first brought Brandon to, the house where I spent my only years as a married woman. I saw a For Sale sign in the yard and found the house vacant, so I pulled in the driveway, got out, and sat on the front steps.

"And I cried. Bawled my ever-loving eyes out, like you did on that baseball field last year. To release over twenty years of pent-up emotion was cleansing, that's for sure. I got mad at myself later for crying over Brandon and tried to convince myself none of this was my fault. It ought to be him crying over what he did to me and especially to our kids. He left, not me.

"But I remembered back to what stood out about Pastor Hobbs' response to his wife's murder. He didn't blame, but he also didn't push forward like it never happened. What I witnessed in the dining room here last year was courage. Pastor, I wanted you to be mad at that man, and it angered me on the inside when you told us you had forgiven him. But you possessed a peace I hoped would find me one day but hadn't yet. As unfair as it seemed, you acted differently from how I would have—different from what I did."

Paula drew a deep breath. "I sat there until dark, but I made a decision before I left. When I got home that night, I looked up Pastor Hobbs' email on his church website—y'all really should update your site, Pastor— and requested an appointment to talk to him about forgiveness. He was glad to hear from me but not too surprised if I read him right.

"Our conversation here was still fresh enough that he recalled most of my story. I told him I wanted to do whatever he had done to find the peace he found in his grief. The sarcastic part of me figured I would get a lot of God answers, but I was okay with that, or I wouldn't have called him. Pastor Hobbs mostly listened, but the man asks probing questions that cut to the core. He made me realize rebellion had ruled my life, even before I left home as a teenager, and it wasn't just against my parents but against God. He talked about the kingdom of God and how God is a benevolent King but how he will pursue us to the point of fight, flight, or surrender. Well, long story short, I had chosen fight and flight in the past, neither of which worked for me, so about a week after I met you all, I chose surrender. I decided if the King of the universe wanted me as one of His own, I would be a fool to turn Him down."

"Now, Paula, you're ready to pursue forgiveness. Let's start with making one list of people whom you need to ask for forgiveness for things you've done or said against them. Make a second list of people who have wronged you that you need to forgive."

"Even if they don't ask?"

"*Especially* if they don't ask."

"As rebellious as I have been, Pastor, I have done a fair job of mending broken relationships, if I say so myself. I learned through interacting with my children, which helped me humble myself to my parents. I did it and our relationship is fine now. They've been wonderful grandparents, so I'm glad I made things right with them."

Pastor Hobbs drummed his fingers together and smiled. They both understood the destination she needed to reach. She recounted mending the fence with her former boss and several more mended relationships. Finally, she stopped and sighed.

"I need to forgive Brandon."

"You realized that all along, didn't you?"

"Yes." A long silence. "I didn't want to say it. If I didn't say it, it wouldn't be real. But there, I said it."

"You did."

"It's not fair," she said flatly.

He smiled, continuing to drum his fingers.

"He ought to be the one asking my forgiveness, Pastor, you must admit that."

"You're right."

Silence.

"But it doesn't matter, does it?"

Silence.

"Because I'm never going to get any peace until I forgive him, am I?"

Silence.

"I don't need to seek him out, though, do I? I can forgive him in my heart. God will give me credit for that, won't He?"

Silence.

"But I suppose I should attempt to locate him and determine if it would be wise to reach out."

Silence.

"I don't do social media, and I'm sure he doesn't either."

Silence.

"But I guess with the internet and a little searching, I should be able to find him."

Silence.

"Chances are, he's not sorry for leaving. If he was, he would have reached out by now, at least to re-connect with his children."

Silence.

"The last thing he'll probably want is to hear from me."

Silence.

"But this is about following God. It's about me forgiving Brandon and releasing him from anything I believe he owes me and getting released from the anger and bitterness I've had toward him all these years."

Silence.

"He might not even say he's sorry."

Silence.

"But I'll have the peace I'm looking for, whether or not he does, right?"

Silence.

"You don't talk much in counseling, do you?"

"I learned some time ago to lead people to Jesus if they don't have a personal relationship with Him and say as little as necessary afterward. Most people who set up counseling understand what they should do before they come visit me. I try to stay quiet long enough for them to say their action step out loud."

"You've done this for a while."

"Yes, ma'am."

"So what should I do?"

"You've already said what you need to do. Pray through everything first, though. If you want any help working through what you should do, call me. I'll be glad to talk you through it."

Paula nodded and grinned. "Or I could go to a nice, quiet place and speak my concerns out loud. I can pause after every sentence, listen to crickets in return, and understand exactly what to do."

Pastor Hobbs allowed himself a smile. Standing, he said, "Yes, I suppose you could do that, too. God is better at counseling than I am."

PAULA MADE eye contact with her children. "I didn't tell you because I wasn't sure what I'd find when I looked for him. Do you want to know what I discovered?"

Lisa and David nodded without thinking.

19

"I started poking around on the internet earlier this year, but I couldn't pick up his scent. I Googled him —nothing. Facebook—nothing. He was skeptical about technology back in the day—paid cash for everything, even when it inconvenienced him. So I made another appointment to talk with Pastor Hobbs, and you'll never believe what he suggested."

"What?" Carol asked, eager to learn where this led.

"He told me to check criminal records."

"That's one tool we use to help folks at the mission search for their relatives when we can't find them any other way," said Pastor Hobbs. "You'd be surprised at how effective it is sometimes."

"Right," Paula continued, "and sure enough, that's where I first found the slightest hint of his trail. All I knew—or thought I did—was he left Mississippi in October 1999, headed to Texas, pulling a bass boat. Like I told y'all last year, I haven't heard a word from him since. To my knowledge, he's never contacted our kids." Lisa and David shook their heads as one.

"So, back to the criminal record. It took a little digging, but I found it and pieced together the better part of his life after he left here. Kids, are y'all sure you want to hear this?" They nodded.

"He hadn't been there six months when the police arrested him for possession with intent to sell in Richardson, Texas, a suburb north of Dallas. According to the arrest report, the police raided the house of a married couple named Stearns in a west-side neighborhood after a tip from a guy caught with drugs in his car. When they entered the house, Brandon was sleeping on the couch, and they arrested him along with them. He went to court, where he convinced the judge he didn't know about the Stearnses' operation, that they had just given him a place to crash after he moved to town. He told the judge he sold a boat after the arrest and rented his own place, and if the judge let him go, he would never see him again. I don't know if Brandon told the truth, but the judge let him off, and he rented his own apartment—all cash deposit and rent. That's why I didn't find a record of his lease on the internet, not even an address."

"How did you find his address?" Tara asked.

"The next entry on his criminal record, a misdemeanor disturbing the peace charge. It seemed like no big deal except he was fighting the Stearns guy who he had been staying with and the case landed in front of the same judge. The judge recognized them and asked what they were fighting about. Larry Stearns said, 'He owes me money.' Stearns and his wife spent five years in prison on the drug charge. He had been out a grand total of three days when he tracked Brandon down at a bar in Richardson and demanded 'his money,' according to what the bartender told police.

"The judge put two and two together. He told Brandon, 'If I remember correctly, you said if I let you off of the other charge, I would never see you in my courtroom again.' Brandon told him he wouldn't have if this Stearns guy hadn't burst into the bar where he was not bothering a soul and picked a fight over money he said Brandon owed him. The judge asked both of them, 'What money are we talking about, gentlemen?'

"The original police report listed the amount of drugs seized in the raid, but it also made note that the cops recovered about two thousand dollars. After the judge read that part of the report, he said, 'Appears an operation like yours, Mr. Stearns, might have left a lot more cash hidden around the house somewhere. Is that the money to which we're referring, gentlemen?' Neither man responded, so the judge turned his attention to Brandon and asked him his address. Brandon rattled off his street address and apartment number. The judge asked how often he frequented the bar where the fight happened. Brandon told him several times a week. He asked if he was drunk on the night in question, and Brandon shook his head, said he was still on his first beer. He added that he normally drank only two or three and walked home. The transcript hinted that the judge was trying to pry something from him, but

Brandon got hung up on the drinking questions and never saw it coming.

"Then the judge asked about his employer. Brandon claimed to be between jobs. The judge pressed and asked him what he did in his last place of employment. He told him he worked on the dock at a trucking company. Then the judge point-blank asked him if he had had a job since he moved to Texas. Brandon told him nothing full-time. The judge quizzed him about the amount of his rent and his regularity in paying it. Brandon answered six hundred dollars and that he paid it on time every month. The judge asked if he made a habit of eating. Brandon laughed and said yes. The judge said he figured with all of his expenses—rent, utilities, food, and two or three beers several times a week at the neighborhood bar—Brandon lived on about $1,500 a month. He asked if that sounded correct, and Brandon answered 'more or less.'

"The judge did some figuring on some paper he had in front of him—this court reporter was good; she caught everything. 'So, Mr. Gull,' he said after a few moments, 'by my math it has cost you approximately $90,000 to live these past five years. More or less. On the income side of the ledger, you do some part-time work that you can't quite put your finger on to earn your living. Are you getting welfare money?" Brandon shook his head. 'Son,' the judge continued, 'those numbers don't add up.' Brandon told him he had sold his boat and his truck. The judge—no lie—said, 'Must have been a yacht to produce five years' living expenses. How did you come to purchase this boat in the first place?' And

Brandon said—are y'all ready for this—'my ex-wife bought it for me.' The judge said he found that difficult to believe, like he found it hard to believe a boat and a truck fetched more or less $90,000. 'So, I'll ask you again, gentlemen: What money were you fighting about?' They didn't answer, and the judge fined them $500 apiece for disturbing the peace and suggested Brandon pay the fine for both of them.

"They must have worked it out somehow because Brandon's name doesn't show up again on the court records for another five years. He was still living in Richardson, and this time they charged him with trespassing on school grounds. According to the arrest report—again, very detailed—he was hanging out by the tennis courts of one of the local high schools. That's near the street, but he was on the school side of the courts, close to the other athletic facilities. The softball field is right there, and the baseball field and track are adjacent. With games going on after school, a teacher taking up admission money suspected him of dealing drugs and called the assistant principal, who arrived about ten minutes later.

"In the time before the principal arrived, several students walked up to Brandon, talked for a few minutes, and left. The teacher didn't say she observed drugs or money change hands from that distance, but their interaction looked suspicious. When the assistant principal arrived, he marched straight to Brandon, who was standing alone by the tennis courts, and asked him his purpose for being there. He responded that he was waiting on some friends to go to the baseball game, but the principal didn't buy it. He walked up the hill to talk to the teacher who had called him. I'm sure Brandon saw them talking, and he probably witnessed the principal pull out his phone and make a call.

"By the time the police arrived, Brandon had moved down to the track to walk laps. The officer told him he needed to leave the school grounds. Brandon argued that all he was doing was taking a walk, just like dozens of other folks out walking that day. The officer gave him the choice of walking off the school campus right away or walking to his patrol car in handcuffs. Brandon put up an argument—not belligerent, according to the report, just stubborn—and the officer arrested him for trespassing.

"He had a different judge this time, thank goodness for him. The judge asked him if the principal told him to leave. Brandon told him the principal's words were that if he didn't have any reason to be there, he needed to move on from school property. Instead, he took a walk on the track since it was such a pretty day. He pointed out that there were forty or fifty other people out there walking, none of whom the police arrested. The judge agreed and threw out the case.

"That's the last entry on Brandon's criminal record. However, I found one other court record involving Brandon Gull, but this time not a criminal case. Not too long ago, he legally changed his name from *Brandon Gull* to *Brandon Wade*. *Wade* is his middle name, so I know it has to be him. I returned to where I started in the first place, looking at public records and social media for *Brandon Wade* this time. Lo and behold, Brandon has discovered technology.

"He has a Facebook page he opened with the crudest of selfie cover photos, but it was clear enough to identify him. It was a profile that screams he is there to look at other people's stuff instead of their looking at his. It made me wonder if he had been checking up on us, but he never tried to connect with us. Anyway, his profile still listed his location as Richardson, Texas. Once I figured all that out, one thing remained: to reach out to him. I didn't want to do it online, and I didn't figure he would respond if I did, so I took a few days off last month and drove to Texas. Lisa, sorry, I didn't really go to the big flea market near Jackson like I told you. I booked a room at a hotel in Garland, which is a town over, so chances were a lot less that I would accidentally bump into Brandon. I wanted to get the lay of the land before I started searching for him.

"I staked out Brandon's apartment complex—if he still lived there—on Friday morning early, like when most people would go to work. I remained skeptical Brandon would be in that crowd. Right around 7:00, though, I saw a clean-cut guy about my age get in an electrical company truck. He wore a work shirt and cap, but besides looking like a contributing member of the workforce instead of a hippie vagabond, I was ninety-five percent convinced it was Brandon.

"If I had planned it better, I would have approached him in the morning when he was rushing to work and couldn't stick around to talk. That way, I could have said my peace, he would have responded one way or the other, and I could have packed my stuff up and headed back to Mississippi. I didn't, though, so I hung out at a coffee shop reading a book for the better part of the morning. I hit one of those burger joints they have out there that we don't in Harriston for lunch. After that, I found a neighborhood park to walk off at least some of lunch before reading some more of my book. At around three-thirty, I headed back to Brandon's apartment complex. I parked next to where his truck was that morning and backed into the spot to be sure to speak first before he recognized me. My windows are tinted enough that he wouldn't notice me through my driver's side window unless he was looking for me. And then I waited. At five-thirty, he turned into the parking lot, drove right to the same parking spot, and pulled straight in. He stepped out of his truck without glancing my way.

20

"Long day?"

"Yeah, it was," Brandon Wade said, turning to locate the female voice. "No. Way. Paula? What are you doing here? How did you find me? "

"Yes way. You don't want to know how I found you, but I'm here to forgive you and let go of the bitterness I have carried since you left."

"Sure, yeah, okay," he scrambled. "Say, I understand if you want to say your peace and go back home, but would you be willing to sit down for a conversation?"

Paula thought for a moment, but her instincts gave way to her curiosity. This fresh-cut version of Brandon intrigued her. "A conversation," she heard herself say.

"Do you mind if I clean up and change into some regular clothes right quick? We can go..."

"Brandon, I'm not having a drink with you," Paula snapped.

"... get a bite to eat," he finished. "There's an

authentic Mexican place two blocks from here." There went her upper hand she had told herself she would maintain.

"Okay, I'll wait."

"You sure?"

"Yeah, I've got a book to read. I'll be fine."

"All right, I'll hurry."

He was back in twenty minutes, sporting jeans, a Texas Rangers T-shirt, and a pair of red Chucks. He smelled better.

"Since when are you into football?"

"The Rangers are the baseball team here in Dallas. Arlington, actually. Some guys from work invited me to a game once."

"Oh, right, Football is the Cowboys, right?" *Strike two, Lord, help me quit sticking my foot in my mouth.*

"Yeah. Believe it or not, I went to one of their games, too. I had to see that stadium everybody's talking about. It's massive. Not that I can compare it to many other sports stadiums, but I can't imagine one any bigger."

"Everything's bigger in Texas, right?"

"So they say. Is Mexican fine with you?"

"Sure."

"Okay, follow me." He gave her the address in case she fell behind. She noticed he drove his work truck and didn't ask to ride in her car. The restaurant was full but not crowded. They grabbed a booth in the corner. She ordered water with lemon and was surprised when he asked for water with lime.

"So, Paula, I'm sure you didn't come out here for

chitchat, so I'll skip the *you're looking great* and all, although you do. Where did you want to start?"

She had rehearsed the speech all the way to Texas and could have said it backward by now. "Brandon, you hurt me when you left and took all our money. It has been a hard life, providing for two kids and trying to give them a chance in life. I lost my job because of you, which could have put us in a big hole and on welfare. But it didn't. You never once reached out about your two children. Honestly, I preferred it that way, but I recently came to recognize the depth of the bitterness I held onto because of what you did to us. I also understand the only way to turn it loose is to forgive you. You don't owe me any explanations or money or future contact or even an apology. I need to do this for me. So, bottom line, Brandon, while what you did hurt me and hurt our children, I forgive you, no strings attached."

Tears filled his eyes as their server approached to take their order. Sensing the levity of the moment, the server said, "I'll give you a few more minutes." Brandon nodded and mouthed *thank you*.

"Paula, that was brave. Thank you. That was something I should have done—asking your forgiveness, that is. I wanted to, but by the time I understood what I had done, I was too ashamed to call. That's no excuse. I've been trying to work my way toward reaching out for the last few months. My bad habits followed me out here and only got worse. I got in some trouble a few months after I got here..." When he caught the slightest of flinches, he smiled and lowered his head. "That's how you found me."

She nodded. "Go on."

"Well, you probably learned the story of my first ten years here then." When she nodded, he continued, "There was fifty thousand dollars under a trap door in that house that the police didn't find. I took it when the couple I was staying with spent time in jail. I burned through most of the money in four years. I realized when they got out of prison, they'd come looking for the money. I should have just moved, tried to start over new somewhere else, but I was stupid and fast running out of money, so I stayed. I went back to this little business I'm not proud of. I nearly got busted when the cops picked me up for trespassing at a high school, but I hid the drugs I was carrying in some hedges by the baseball field. I came back to the track, where they eventually arrested me. I dealt drugs long enough to pay the guy back everything I owed him. On the day I payed him back, plus interest, I walked to the barbershop, got a haircut, and started looking for a reputable job. I haven't dealt or used drugs since."

Their server slowed down as she neared their table, ready to make another quick exit. Brandon waved her over. "Steak fajitas for me." Paula ordered brisket tacos, and the server spun away toward the kitchen.

"I came across this guy who leads a recovery ministry. He owns the electrical company I work for, and he believed me when I told him I was looking to make a fresh start. He has taken chances on a lot of guys in recovery and gotten burned a few times, so I recognized what a chance he was taking. He started me on the paperwork the next week and bought me a little time before I had to take a drug test, which I passed. I wasn't making much when I started, but he gave me some overtime work and made sure I had a ride to and from work until he promoted me and gave me a company truck.

"I wasn't lying to that judge about selling my boat and my truck, though not exactly in the manner I told him. Anyway, my job has allowed me to pay my bills and put back a little for a house in a better part of town or something of my own to drive. I was planning to come back to Mississippi to find you and apologize for all I've done when I bought a car. Step nine of recovery is to make amends as much as possible. There's no way I can go back and change things with you or with Lisa and David, but perhaps I could help now, maybe with Lisa's wedding."

"How did you know about her engagement?"

"Facebook. I guess I'm what you call a lurker."

Part of Paula wanted to still be mad with him. But the voice inside her head reminded her of the great lengths she took to make this trip to put her bitterness in her rearview mirror. Instead of the snide comment that would have come so naturally mere weeks before, she held out her hand. "Give me your phone." He reluctantly put it in her hand. "Smile," she said, snapping a photo as soon as he did. "Now go update that atrocious profile pic of yours."

For the first time since she asked about the length of his workday, Brandon relaxed a little. "So I'm not the only Facebook lurker?"

"Just trying to find you. Probably better you didn't

put a phone number on your profile, or I might have just called instead of coming out here to face you myself."

"I'm glad you're here. I wish I had come back to Mississippi years ago."

"I would've knocked you all the way back to Texas."

"I would have deserved it, too. Paula, I am truly sorry for everything I put you and Lisa and David through. I sometimes think back and wonder if it might have worked out differently. There's one thing in particular I wish I could do over. The night you told me you were pregnant for the first time, I mentioned to my friend Bubba... do you remember?"

"You said we might go church the next morning. I got up early and cooked breakfast in case you were serious."

"You remember. My brain was so foggy back then and for years afterward, but that night I remember. I was ready to change everything for our baby, and I figured that was the place to start, but then I just... didn't. I tried to figure out why I didn't go. I wonder how things might have changed. We might have followed God's plan for marriage and parenting and made new friends. I might have stopped drinking so much and kept my job. You obviously would have kept yours."

"Guess we'll never know."

"No, I reckon not." His downcast expression seemed genuinely sad, and Paula felt a tiny pang of compassion for him. She fought the urge to reach across and put her hand on his. Their food arrived, and the moment passed.

Brandon and Paula ate in silence for a few minutes, save for an occasional grunt or mouth-filled "Mm, this is good." Finally, Brandon sat upright, laid his fork on his plate and asked, "Would you mind telling me about Lisa and David? If you don't want to, I'll understand."

Paula was almost finished with her first taco, so she took time to finish it and to consider how much she wanted to share. He had not once called them *my kids* or *our kids*. That might have brought an abrupt end to the conversation, but he seemed to be respectful of her and cognizant of his lack of rights to any information about the children he had fathered.

"What do you know?"

"Not a lot. They seem like private people, at least online. Lisa will graduate college and get married, all in one day. I hope that day is everything she wants it to be. David served our country in the army and is quite the young entrepreneur. He is generous with his money."

She couldn't hide a scowl.

"No, Paula, no, I wouldn't dare," he inserted before her thoughts ran away. "I was talking about your beach trip, Lisa's engagement and all."

I've got to stop jumping to conclusions. "Oh, sorry."

"It's okay. You've got every right. I was just going to say that I'm glad you finally got to take your trip to the beach. You've earned it. Lisa and David seem like wonderful people. You did good, Paula."

"Thanks." She allowed a slight smile at this acknowledgement. For most of the last two decades, she would have filled him in on everything his *you did good* included, highlighting the absent father part of the equation. Not tonight.

"Lisa is quiet and thoughtful, very smart. She paid her way through college with scholarships, studied hard, and met the man she's going to marry. What could be better than that, right? Jake's a keeper, too. We love him. For him to consider our family enough to include us—especially David—in his proposal to Lisa was beyond special. I enjoyed meeting his family, too. I was a little nervous before our trip, but they're good people, normal folks. Lisa has earned everything that's come her way, and I couldn't be prouder of her or happier for her.

"David didn't do quite as well in school, mainly because he found his interest in his yard cutting business. I tell you what, that fits him. He works hard and takes a lot of pride in the work he does. His customers love him, too. I tell you what convinced me he had found his passion, though, was when he started hiring people. He didn't wait until he needed help and then hire the first one of his friends to step forward. No, he developed quite a vetting process when he hired his first helper at sixteen. The kids—I call them kids, but *young men* would be a better term—who ran his business while he was gone were mirror images of David. To me, that was a testament to how he trained them. He pays them well and expects them to deliver the best customer service of anybody in the business.

"I figured he would finish high school and make great money right off the bat by cutting yards full time. It wasn't a problem for him to expand—Brandon, he has a waiting list of people who want to hire him. That's unheard of in the grass cutting business, I hear. Anyway, he loves our country and wanted to serve a tour of duty in the army. He did his three years, saved about everything he made, and now he's ready to go to college to get a business degree to go along with running the business he already has. His plan is to expand gradually until he's finished with college and devote all his time to it or possibly start another business."

21

Brandon listened while Paula continued to brag on both children. When she paused, he mumbled, "I'm glad neither of them turned out like me." He said it so quietly that Paula had to ask him to repeat it. When he did, she noticed a tear trickling down his face.

"I'll be honest with you, that has been one of my biggest fears all these years. Brandon, I'm not looking to pile on. I can tell you're carrying regrets. Until recently, that's what I wanted most for you. But last year I met a group of folks, and they said some things that made me reflect on life and myself. One guy in the group experienced a meltdown on his way to the restaurant where we all met. It was years in the making, but to the rest of us listening to his story, it seemed inevitable. When I considered the anger and bitterness and defensiveness I've been carrying far longer than he had, I figured if I didn't deal with it soon, the next meltdown would be mine.

"There was a pastor in our group, too. His wife had been murdered by a homeless man she tried to help. The way he described his wife, she seemed like an angel, a person who loved all kinds of people and whom everybody loved. To be shot serving homeless people—what a despicable act. And yet, this pastor told her story all calm and composed on his first Thanksgiving without her. I was angry, I'll tell you. Angry. Angry at the man who killed her. Angry at this pastor for not being angry with the man who killed his wife. He forgave him instead, even took a Thanksgiving meal to the jail for him. Who does that, right?

"And yet, as I shared my story, I realized I had far less to be angry about than he did. When those folks started telling me what a great mother I had been, I didn't accept it. Then, they began pointing out character qualities they saw in my kids through the stories I told about them. I focused on keeping food on the table and on my fear that they would take a sudden right turn like..." Paula choked on the next words, ones she had never considered.

"Like their old man?" Brandon offered.

"Like their mother. I've never really put it together before, but I had great parents, two wonderful people. They gave me everything I needed and a lot of what I wanted, but that was never enough for me. All they asked in return was respect. When I turned sixteen, I decided I wouldn't give it to them anymore, that I would make my own way in the world. Brandon, all this time, I thought I feared they would turn out like you, but it was me I most feared they would follow. I'm sorry."

"You didn't want them turning out like me, either. I chewed on my own way until I finally choked on it. You would assume nobody would look out for my best interests better than me, but when I've tried to control my own life, I've messed it up every time. Paula, the truth is, when I left, I didn't leave you and our kids as much as I ran from myself. I'm not making excuses—what I did was wrong and without excuse—but the weight of the responsibility I was about to have, a son—it overwhelmed me. I convinced myself both of our kids would be better off without ever remembering me. It was a coward's way out. I was wrong and I'm sorry. When I started to turn my life around—more to the point, by the time God began turning my life around—I had no right. I accept that, and you need not worry about me trying to show up where I'm not wanted.

"Brandon, I…"

"Don't respond. I'm not looking to push you toward anything. I understand you came out here to release me from anything I owe you, and I totally respect and admire that. I have no desire to complicate matters. So let's leave it here, okay? I accept your forgiveness, even if I don't believe you have anything to forgive. And I want to say again, loud and clear, how wrong I was to bail on you. I was more wrong to take everything that was far more yours than mine, and even more wrong to leave you to support what should have been our children to raise." His tears flowed freely now, and she fought her own. She had never imagined this kind of response from a career freeloader.

"Paula, let me say, though, you have been—you are —an amazing mother. I'm glad you found a group of people to tell you as much. You deserve it. Lisa and David are a testament to how hard you've worked to give them a life they never would have had if I had stayed. One thing I would ask you to consider on your drive back to Mississippi: If there's any kind of restitution I could make, you just name it."

"Brandon, I—"

He waved her off. "Don't answer now. Consider it."

"Brandon, I'm not starting that cycle of unforgiveness over again. I forgive you. You don't owe us a thing."

"So... Mom, how did y'all leave it?" Lisa was fighting tears, holding Jake's hand to her right and David's to her left.

"With a clean slate. We both wiped away many years of regrets, some we didn't even realize we had. I'll be honest, I'm not sure how it would have gone if he didn't seem so... different. Tara, he must have been going through the same steps you talked about earlier. Seems like he was stuck where you said many people in recovery are."

"Restitution," Tara said.

"Yeah, I believe he has been ready to talk forgiveness for a while, but he couldn't imagine what twenty years of staying away would look like as far as restitution. I tried my best to relieve him of that because I seriously didn't go out there to get anything from him. I haven't wanted anything for years. What I did want was to hear him say what he did was wrong, but I'm no longer interested in seeing him wallow in it. Anyway, when I saw the changes he has already made, it prepared me to accept what he said about wanting to reach out but not knowing what would be appropriate. I've gone down multiple bad roads by taking him at his word in the past, so I made myself wait before allowing more than forgiveness. We have texted a few times since then, and he seems to still be doing well. He earned a raise and more responsibility at work, so that continues to trend in a positive direction. I hope he can finally get out of that dump of an apartment complex where he has lived all these years. I only saw it from the outside, and I can only imagine what it looks like after twenty years of his living there. He never helped with housework at our house, but maybe that has changed, too. Who knows?"

"Mom, do you think..." Lisa started but stopped, looking around the room. "Perhaps we should talk about it after..."

"Go ahead. You might as well ask in front of my best friends here. Do I think what?"

David finished the question when Lisa hesitated again. "... he would want a relationship with us?"

"You would want that?"

"He is our father," David said. "I've never met him, and Lisa doesn't remember him at all. But I'm sure I speak for both of us when I say we don't want to do anything to make you uncomfortable. I mean, you're our mom and you've been the one who has been there for us all these years. But if he has changed as much as you say, you know, perhaps it's time?"

"I haven't told you because I wanted to protect you if all this is not real. Plus, I didn't want to get anyone's hopes up in case either of you didn't want to pursue a relationship. This wasn't exactly the setting I had in mind to broach the subject, but there you have it. You might as well tell me how you feel."

David and Lisa stared at each other and reached a decision without saying a word, nodding in unison. Without noticing she was doing so, Paula bobbed her head up and down, too. "It's decided, then. I'll call your dad soon and see if he's ready to, well, *meet* you, really."

The room grew quiet until Lisa asked in a hushed tone, "Mom, do you think there's any chance Dad might come to my wedding?"

"You would want that?"

"No. And yes. What I mean is, I don't want him to be there because of any part he has played in my life. David will still walk me down the aisle and you will still stand with me as my maid of honor. Even though those are weird roles for y'all to be playing, it fits who we are as a family. But, if we develop a relationship with Dad, I want to look back and remember he came to my wedding. If not, at least we tried, right?"

"Well, I can make a call if that's what you desire, but you and Jake should chat about this in private, and you, me, and David could talk later, too?"

"Sure."

"Any other surprises to throw at us tonight, Paula?" Carol called from the back.

"Like what?"

"Oh, like the guy in 4A?"

"Oh, heavens no."

"Some nice fella at work?"

"No."

"Well, how about... some... guy... in Texas?"

"What? No. Uh, no."

Laticia turned around and shook her head. "Ms. Carol, you love a nice love story, don't you, even if you need to invent one?"

Carol flushed. "Yes, I suppose I do. I'm sorry, Paula, I stepped over the line. You're such a wonderful person who I would love to see happy in a relationship."

"Thank you, Ms. Carol, but I'm still focused on getting my baby girl married. You can use all your being happy for me on her."

CAROL

22

"Y ou next." Paula pointed to Carol. "I've said more than enough. Time for you to take the hot seat... well, the hot stand, I guess."

Carol walked to the front of the room, pulling her husband with her. "Everybody, this is Irv, he of the inconvenient heart attack. This year has been unbelievable for us. After Irv came home the Saturday after Thanksgiving, he proved a champ at rehab. He's got a sweet-looking scar, but otherwise, he's seems healthier than ever."

"Want to see it?" Irv asked the crowd, grabbing the bottom of his shirt and feigning a tug.

"Stop it, dear." Carol put her hand on his. "He's proud of his scar."

"This is an expensive scar, physically and financially. It's also a daily reminder of the tragedy that could have been. When I look in the mirror, I consider what I still want to teach my sons and how I want to protect my two girls from any boys not worthy of them." He shot a stern glance at the two young men sitting with his daughters. They smiled back, used to the spiel.

"Oh, cut it out, tough guy," Carol said. "You know good and well if these young men were brave enough to approach our daughters and honorable enough to pass the muster with their brothers, they are a special breed. Fellas, y'all stand up and let me introduce you to our friends." First, Carol motioned to the wavy-haired blonde, athletic-looking one. "This is Garen, Beth's boyfriend." Turning to the tall, thin, brown-headed young man, she said, "And this is Michael, Kate's boyfriend." Carol smiled sweetly and thanked them for letting her embarrass them.

"After Irv started physical therapy, we decided as a family to establish better eating habits and to start exercising on a regular basis. The kids stay active, but Irv and I began the habit of taking a thirty-minute walk every evening after supper, even in cold weather. When we heard about a 5K run coming up at the end of April, we stepped it up a notch and signed up for it. By late March we had worked up to half jogging and half walking. Irv felt great, and his doctor bragged on his progress. I wanted to surprise Irv by asking the rest of our family to join us for the race, to rally around him and celebrate that he was still with us. The kids could have run a 5K on any given day, so they didn't require time to train.

"Anyway, the day of the 5K arrived and Irv and I rose early and ate a nutritious breakfast. We drove downtown well before the race since we had never done

one of these before. We attached our bibs to the front of our running outfits we had bought for the occasion. Thirty minutes before the race, I told Irv we should start stretching, but I did that so the kids would stand a better chance of sneaking up on him and surprising him. It worked, too. They checked in, attached their bibs, and walked over to where we were bent over stretching before Irv ever suspected a thing.

"So, we started running the race, and Irv and I didn't even try to keep pace with the young people. They disappeared from sight by the second or third turn. Irv and I kept an even pace since our goal was to finish, even if we had to walk sometimes. As we started our last mile, we saw Isaiah and Jeremiah running the wrong way toward us. They had crossed the finish line already and wanted to come back to finish with Irv. We ran another half mile, and Beth and Kate joined us after completing their races. Aliyah and Rebecca came back for the last quarter mile, and we all crossed the line together. All four of our kids finished top three in their age groups and won medals. Guess who else won a medal?"

Irv grabbed his wife by the wrist and held her hand aloft. "Carol Turner, first in her age group with a time of 36:07."

"Ahead of nobody else in the age 50-59 female division. Several retired ladies in their sixties and seventies and plenty of younger moms pushing strollers ran circles around me, but I showed up on a day when every other woman runner in my age group had something better to do."

"Dear, I keep telling you," Irv interrupted, "that you shouldn't give all the specifics. Bask in the glow of your first-place medal."

"Oh, I don't care about any medals. We won the day by surprising you."

"Well, you did that, for sure. When I looked up and saw our crew coming, I just about had a heart att—ooh, maybe not the best analogy. Regardless, it was outstanding to share the experience with everybody else."

"But we had more family running the race with us than we thought," Carol said. "We had a big party over at Isaiah and Aliyah's house afterward to celebrate Irv's graduation from physical therapy and for all of us finishing the race. After we cheered for Irv, Isaiah told us he and Aliyah wanted to share some news with us. Are y'all ready? On the same day I finished first in my age group in my first 5K, I discovered I am going to be a grandmother!" Carol squealed as the cheers began.

"Well, Ms. Carol," Paula said, "you have had one magical year."

"In a lot of ways, yes. But this summer—not so much. We knew my mother had dementia. It started about a year-and-a-half ago, and at first her issues were ever so slight. She would forget things, but we always picked at her about being forgetful, anyway. As a mother of two sets of twins, I did my share of forgetting along the way, so I didn't pay enough attention to Mom's loss of memory. One day, though, she wandered from home, and nobody had any idea where she had gone. My dad passed away several years ago, but she had neighbors who checked up on her. They searched for her in her usual places—church, grocery story, senior citizen community center. They called the police, who found her three blocks away, sitting on somebody's front porch. She said she was waiting on friends to return from the post office with her package, but when the people drove up, they told the policemen they had never even met Mom. She hadn't eaten or drunk anything in at least ten hours, so she was quite disoriented.

"We recognized it was past time to do something. With our being four hours away, we couldn't look after her to the degree she needed. I didn't have any brothers or sisters to help care for her, and she would have given up if we ever put her in a home. It didn't take Irv and me long to determine our only viable option was to bring her to live with us. Our house is plenty big since the boys moved out, although we had to make some adjustments to produce a more dementia-proof home for her. Mom would enjoy a semblance of independence, and we could keep a better eye on her. I would cut back showing houses, but now that those hungry boys are buying their own groceries, we don't need my income anymore, anyway.

"Our plan worked, in theory, but the reality of the last few months is that I've been chasing a toddler around, only one who could open doors and walk away. This one didn't believe she should tell you where she was going. This one drove a car for so many years that she assumed she had a right to take my keys and drive my car. Like a toddler, she didn't respond well to *stop* and *no*. Some things she would say to us would have been hilarious if she hadn't been my mother who raised me and taught me so much about life."

Carol stopped, giggling to herself. "Okay, I will tell you about this one time. We had just eaten breakfast. Irv kissed me goodbye and headed off to work. Mom kissed me, too, and walked down the hall to her room to brush her teeth, like she did every morning. I cleaned up after breakfast, like I did every morning. Our routine was that when I finished cleaning the kitchen, I knocked on Mom's door, and she joined me for a walk around the neighborhood. Only this time, Mom didn't follow her routine. That's the thing with dementia patients—they might follow their routine a thousand times in a row, and one day, without warning, they fly off the radar.

"On the morning to which I'm referring, I tapped on Mom's door, and she didn't answer, so I knocked a little louder. When she still didn't answer, I cracked the door to see what was keeping her. She wasn't there or in her bathroom. I looked all over the house before I noticed the front door was cracked. Right there on the front porch, I found the cap she was wearing at breakfast that morning. It wasn't hard to tell which direction she headed, either. I found a shoe on the sidewalk in front of the house and a bright pink sock about a hundred feet south in the direction we always walked. Another hundred feet, another shoe. Another hundred feet, another sock. She must have counted steps or some-thing, because everything was so evenly spaced out.

"I panicked a little when I saw her belt at the corner where we turn to walk toward a neighborhood park near there. A hundred feet later, I picked up Mom's blouse, followed by her shorts at the entrance of the park. I'm sure I appeared funny carrying all of my mother's clothes into the park, but it scared me to death what I might find next. I looked up to see my mother jogging laps around the fountain in the center of the park, wearing nothing but her underclothes. I've got to tell you, by that point I considered it a win for her to still be wearing anything at all." Everyone in the room lost every measure of restraint they had tried to keep for Carol's sake, and she encouraged them to let it out. "I know, it's sad but also funny as all get out. Thank goodness she didn't draw an audience in the park, nor did she give me any trouble about putting her clothes back on and walking her home. She kept saying she wanted to be like that blonde thing, like that pretty blonde thing. Well, it turns out the blonde thing to which she referred was a teenage girl sunbathing in her backyard across the street and wearing a bikini. Mom saw her through the open gate to her backyard and got her pretty blonde thing going."

"Oh, you've got to stop," Paula said, clutching her side. "I'm sorry for laughing, but..." She doubled over again.

"Mom was an attractive young lady in her time," Carol said, wiping tears away from her eyes and trying to finish the story amidst the laughter now filling the room. "She colored her hair blonde a time or two, and it worked for her—better than it did for me. She made a cute little old lady in her golden years. But I had to break it to her that she would never again have the body of the pretty blonde thing, and that keeping her clothes on needed to be a priority."

Irv leaned over and whispered something in Carol's ear. She nodded and announced, "Okay, since you enjoyed that Mom story, I'll share another. This one is more G-rated. First, I need to tell you that my mom has done crossword puzzles for as far back as I remember. She has a better grasp on the English language and vocabulary than anybody I know. She forgot many things, but not words. At least not until she moved in with us. She started using words close to what she intended, but not quite. She would say... oh, Irv, what's an example?"

Irv laughed. "One night, we were sitting around the dinner table, safe inside our usual routine, and Martha blurted, 'I'm boring.' She often complained she was imposing on us, and we would have to convince her she was welcome in our home. Usually, all she wanted was to help around the house so she would feel needed. The 'I'm boring' statement threw us for a loop, though. It took Carol and me a second to respond. I started telling her about all the interesting things she had done in her life and how many compelling stories she had. Normally, she responded well enough to our efforts to encourage her, but she acted frustrated with me this time. Carol tried to remind her of all the unique skills and crafts she has taught herself through the years, but that was a non-starter, too. When we stopped talking and exchanged a helpless glance, she rolled her eyes at us and said, 'Look, I might be old and forgetful, but you could at least start a movie.' At last Carol and I figured out her mother meant she was *bored* instead of *boring.*"

"This other time," Carol added, "Mom and I had baked a cake on Saturday night for Sunday lunch, when the entire family would be there. Mom came into the kitchen on Sunday morning before church and caught me sneaking a piece of cake. Mom intended to tell me I was *busted.* Instead, she said, 'You're *buxom.*' Irv walked in right behind her and didn't miss a beat. He said, 'Hmm, I've always considered you petite. Better lay off the cake.'"

Irv and Carol grinned as their audience laughed along with them before Carol grew serious. "The same night, she looked me dead in the eye and said, 'Stop living in sin and marry that man.'"

23

"I'm sorry, what?"

"You heard me, Carol. This was not the way Robert and I raised you. I'm going to give you a chance to make it right and marry than man, or I will tell your father. One week, young lady."

"Mom, Irv and I *are* married. We have four children."

"Oh, I realize that. But if he can't make an honest woman out of you—and I mean real soon—I will tell Robert. You can take that to the bank."

"Mom, do you mind if we sit down at the breakfast table?"

"Sure, honey. I understand this is a hard time for you."

Carol took her mother's hands as they sat. "Mom, look at me. Dad died several years ago. He's gone, Mom. Robert's not here."

"Oh, sure, honey, but when he gets back, you, me,

and him are going to have a come-to-Jesus meeting if you don't take care of this."

Carol attempted to maintain control. "Look me in the eyes, Mom. Tell me your name."

"Oh, don't be silly, Karen."

"Mom, my name is Carol."

"That's what I said."

"You called me Karen."

"Karen, Carol—close enough."

"Mom, who am I? Do you recognize me?"

"Of course I recognize who you are, honey. Why would you ask me that?"

"Tell me."

"Carol—your name is Carol."

"Yes, but who am I?"

"You're my… my… sister."

Carol opened her mouth to correct her mother, but when she glimpsed the abject helplessness in her mother's eyes, she stopped short. "Sure, Mom," she whispered, more to herself than anything, "the sister you never had."

Irv walked in after walking Jeremiah and Rebecca to their car. His wife's pleading eyes beckoned him to the table.

"Now, you're going to get it, missy," Martha snapped. "Robert, I need to tell you something. Perhaps you should sit down." Irv's eyes shifted back and forth between the two ladies. Carol offered him a quick shrug, but her eyes told the actual story. They both realized this day would come, and they understood Martha's memory was fading fast, but this still seemed sudden.

Irv sat down and placed his hand on Martha's fore-arm. "Why don't you tell me what's going on, and I'll do what I can to help."

"This... this... hussy... has been living in sin right under our noses, Robert. She acts like she's married—she even has four children—but she's not, Robert, I tell you she's not. I gave her the chance to marry him before you got back from your trip, but she refused. Do something about it."

"Yes, ma'am, I will. Why don't you go to bed and let me take care of this one?"

"You're such a good boy," she said, patting his arm.

MARTHA'S BEDROOM door barely clicked before Carol fell into Irv's arms. Her sobs stayed silent so as not to alarm her mother or her daughters, but they were profound. Irv held her for fifteen minutes before she uttered a word. When she did, Carol had already turned the corner from grief to action. "What are we going to do?"

"Let's give her the night. Perhaps she wakes up in the morning and doesn't remember a thing. Take her to her neurologist's appointment Monday afternoon and listen to what he says. One day at a time, okay? We realized we would endure tough days, and this has been one for all of us. Why don't you tell me the entire conversation and then let's put this day behind us, okay?"

Carol nodded and sank into the couch, where she recounted the bizarre dialogue with her mother. Irv listened, nodded, and smiled at all the right times. He dared not laugh.

"Irv, we understand where this is headed. We believed the doctors when they told us one day she wouldn't recognize us. I thought the doctors and our research prepared me, but I'm not ready, Irv, I'm just not. What if she's not improved in the morning or the doctor can't do anything to help her? What are we going to do?"

"I can make an honest woman of you," Irv said, winking at his wife of thirty years.

———

"AND THAT'S WHAT HE DID," Carol said. "Mom woke up the next morning and scolded me again for living in sin with 'that man,' as she continued to refer to Irv, while at the same time thinking he was her husband. The neurologist ran some tests, and he cautioned us that Mom could be headed downhill fast. That was devastating to hear, but looking back now, we should have seen it coming. For whatever reason, Mom didn't fall much like so many dementia patients do. If she had, we might have been more prepared, but I'm glad her body stayed intact, anyway.

"They wore Mom out with all the questions at the doctor's office, so she remained super quiet when we got home that afternoon. She barely touched her supper and went right to bed afterward. It alarmed us when she didn't come to breakfast the next morning, and we found her in bed, awake but still groggy. Again, very unusual, out of her routine. Irv stayed home from work to help me with her that day, and he convinced her to come eat a little breakfast. She stayed sullen, like she had something heavy on her mind, and she wouldn't look at me. I would ask her questions, and she would tell Irv what to say to me. I was about to have a come apart when Irv left the table and walked toward our bedroom. I figured he was going to brush his teeth and come back in a minute, so I stared at Mom until she finally looked up at me. When I asked her what was wrong, she started crying and shook her head without saying a word.

"Irv came walking back down the hall wearing the shirt Mom always said she liked best, a white button-down with blue pinstripes. She perked up and told him how much she liked it—as if complimenting him on it for the first time. After Irv thanked her, he asked if he might have a word with her in private. I'm telling y'all, my mother responded like he was the President of the United States asking her advice on a critical issue. She carried herself to the front door like... like she was *needed*. They didn't stay outside long, but when they walked through the door, I noticed Mom fighting tears. I thought Irv might have scolded her, but I knew him better than that. I wondered if he said something she took the wrong way. She was letting Irv guide her back to her chair at the breakfast table, though, so I figured he had avoided offending her.

"Irv helped Mom to the table, patted her on the back, and asked if she was ready. She nodded and started crying again. Before I could ask what was going on, Irv dropped to a knee and popped open a little jewelry box and asked me to marry him. Inside the box, where Mom couldn't see it, he had taped a piece of paper that read 'AGAIN.' Y'all, when I squealed, I wasn't acting for my mother." Carol slipped her arm around Irv's waist and squeezed. "This man took the worst couple of days of my life—watching my mother go downhill so fast—and transformed me into a love-struck college girl again. Plus, he honored my mother's biggest wish, even though she was speaking out of her mind.

"We talked to the girls that night about their grand-mother's rapid deterioration and our plan to placate her. I'm telling you, they took the idea and ran with it. Within a week-and-a-half, they planned the whole shebang, even making their own bridesmaid dresses. Mom had taught them how to sew when they were little, so it was so sweet to see that coming full circle. The boys and their wives jumped on board, too. We made sure Mom was okay with Irv having two best men and me having two maids of honor. She called it a *capital* idea—her word—so we wouldn't be showing any favoritism toward any of the children. The entire time, she never lost sight of Irv and me having four children, two sets of twins, two boys and two girls. It was the fact that we had been married for thirty years she couldn't grasp.

"Kate and Beth planned the wedding for our back-yard on a Saturday afternoon. They had already started stringing lights during the week when I had this sneaking suspicion Mom might not stand for a home wedding 'to make an honest woman out of me.' I convinced the girls to ask her instead of me. She pulled them in close—her own granddaughters, mind you—and whispered that if we got married in a church after all these years, the walls would probably fall down. They all enjoyed a girly giggle out of it, but I admit it hurt my feelings to be the object of scorn in this charade. Irv was so gentle in reminding me at every turn how real all this was in Mom's mind. Deep down, I believed that, but it's hard to let go of the mother you've known all your life. Plus, Irv and I were very careful to remain honorable before we married. Anyway, I recognized Mom would not be with us much longer and that I would look back a year later and be glad I did it. I also understood from being right here last Thanksgiving what even the smallest act of kindness can mean.

"Well, Saturday came, and we did it. Irv made an honest bride out of me. He even slept in Jeremiah's old bedroom on Friday night and stayed upstairs the next morning so we wouldn't see each other until the ceremony. When I took in all that Kate and Beth had put together in such a short time, it occurred to me that I gave them a blank check to pay for it. It didn't matter what I thought, though, because I found out later that Irv's financial instructions to them were 'whatever it takes.' They rented those little white chairs for outdoor weddings and a tent for the reception. We had a bride's cake and a groom's cake, flowers galore, and a stringed-instrument quartet. The guys wore tuxedos and the mother of the bride and me wore custom-made dresses compliments of my bridesmaids—my beautiful daughters." Carol paused, taking in the scene in her mind one more time. "Irv, you finish. I like how you tell it best."

Irv cleared his throat. "As much as I wanted to see everything the girls had planned coming to life in our backyard, I made myself stay upstairs on the front side of the house. It helped when the boys arrived about mid-morning, and I talked to them to pass the hours before it was time to get dressed for the ceremony and take our places. Carol was in our bedroom with Martha and Beth and Kate, and I have to admit, when I imagined my bride behind that door, the butterflies in my stomach fluttered."

Carol clasped her hands and folded them under her chin. "See why I have him tell it?"

Irv continued, "The girls invited about a hundred friends and family members to attend our re-wedding, as we call it, and asked a pastor from our church to perform the ceremony. When I looked out our back door and saw everything they had done for us, I about lost it. I made my way around the crowd and took my place behind a giant oak tree to wait for my turn. The music started, and Isaiah walked Martha down the little center aisle to her seat on the front row of the bride's side. The boys joined me and we took our place next to the pastor. The next part—well, let's just say I'm glad they had already repaired my heart."

Carol beamed and said, "I love how he puts that."

"When Kate walked down the aisle, it was like watching a taller version of Carol coming toward me thirty years earlier. Same with Beth. It's not the best phrase for somebody who has had a heart attack to use, but I felt my heart would explode. Everything grew quiet for a few seconds after Beth reached her spot, and they started playing 'Here Comes the Bride.' Everybody stood, and there was that moment of anticipation for everybody, but especially for me."

Carol interrupted again, settling her arm around Irv's waist. "This is my favorite part."

"Mine, too. The door opened and there she stood. Even though the setting differed greatly from our church wedding, my response to seeing Carol was similar. I felt a tingling from my head to my toes. She looked so graceful walking down the hill toward our little makeshift chapel. That won't mean much to you, but she almost face planted at our first wedding. Anyway, as she walked closer, I leaned over and told the pastor I felt as nervous as our first time. He cracked a joke to calm me down, and I relaxed a bit. When Carol was almost to the front, Jeremiah stepped out, and she took his arm. The pastor asked who gave this woman to be wed, and with a straight face, Jeremiah said, 'Her ma and me.' I couldn't believe he said it, and I nearly split my pants laughing so hard. Right up through the rehearsal dinner at our first wedding, Carol's dad insisted that's how he would answer the question. I glanced at Martha, who almost fell out of her chair laughing. I think the pastor was the only one not in stitches, and he would have been, too, if he had been familiar with our family's inside joke.

"We went through the rest of the ceremony with all due seriousness and enjoyed a *lovely* reception." Irv exchanged a playful glance with his daughters in the back of the room. "Girls, it was just *lovely*. We ate cake, drank punch, and danced. Isaiah and Jeremiah danced with their mother, and I danced with our daughters and with Martha. I tell you, by the time we were supposed to leave for our honeymoon, I was plumb tuckered out. However, a honeymoon has a way of giving a man his second wind."

Carol swatted him on the arm. "Oh, stop it. We had a nice honeymoon, though."

"No, dear," Irv corrected, "it was a *lovely* honeymoon."

"He keeps saying that because my mother used the word *lovely* to describe everything at the wedding. The dresses were *lovely*. The ceremony and reception were *lovely*. The decorations—collectively and individually—all *lovely*. She even told the pastor and his wife they looked *lovely*. We don't hear anyone say the word now without thinking of Mom.

"I didn't know about the honeymoon until it was almost time to leave for it," Irv continued. "Neither did Carol. The kids were afraid we wouldn't leave Martha for a night and go. They all planned on staying at the house to watch after her, though, so we figured they could handle her for one night. Carol did her best to stay focused on us, but she worried a lot, even though we only drove two hours away to Mobile."

"Every time I said something about Mom out loud, Irv reeled me in, reminding me the kids had everything under control and that Mom would have a *lovely* time with them. We stayed at a beautiful old downtown hotel, ate delicious seafood, and spent quality time by ourselves for the first time since my mother came to live with us. Taking everything into account, the experience was nothing short of…"

"*Lovely*," the audience said in unison.

Carol hugged Irv again before growing serious. "When we returned home the next day, Mom was super glad we were back. We asked her if everything was okay, and she said it was. We asked her if she had a good time with the kids, and she assured us she had. She started toward her bedroom but looked back at Irv and said, 'Robert, don't let her slip away. Make an honest woman out of her.'

"I cried myself to sleep that night. Mom kept making similar comments, even when the pictures from the wedding—the re-wedding—arrived. I would tell her Irv had already made an honest woman out of me, twice, and show her pictures from both weddings. I would point out pictures of her and Dad from our first wedding and say, 'There's you and Dad. There's Robert.' She would nod and smile and tell me how happy that made her. Still, the next time she saw Irv, it started all over again. I understand it was the disease talking over Mom's memory, but it broke my heart."

24

"Mom passed away almost three months ago. She stayed with us until she died, which was a blessing. Her doctor told us to be ready, and she had an angel of a home health care nurse who sang old hymns to Mom while she cared for her. She must have sung "When We All Get to Heaven" thirty or forty times during Mom's last two weeks. After she indicated Mom's time was near, our family gathered around her when she let go and crossed over. I have heard horror stories from friends of mine whose parents lived with dementia for years and suffered plenty in their last days. Mom's passing was peaceful and pain free.

"The morning before she died, she was as coherent as she had been in months. It seemed she understood her time was short, and so did we. She reminded us she loved Jesus and not to worry about her after she left, that she would be in a much better place. The nurse told us to make our goodbyes as brief as possible. Inside our window of opportunity, we individually told her we loved her, we loved Jesus, too, and we would see her soon. Before Mom slipped into the sleep that she would never come out of, she looked Irv dead in the eye and said, 'Irv, thank you for taking good care of my baby.' The Lord couldn't have picked words we needed to hear more. Not long after that, she stopped breathing, and her race was over."

The group moaned and expressed their condolences. Pastor Hobbs said, "My father lived his last two years with dementia. The circumstances can be varied, but it always seems to go better for patients surrounded by the familiarity of family, even when they don't recognize us for who we are. Carol and Irv, kids—it can be a thankless job to care for someone who doesn't even recognize you. Our parents and grandparents loved us before we had anything to offer them back. It speaks well of us when we love them past when they have anything to give us. Well done, you guys."

"Thank you, Pastor," Carol said on behalf of her family. She noticed Vicki Stapleford took Pastor Hobbs's hand and squeezed it. She looked forward to hearing their story next. But first, she had one more surprise for the group. "One more story and I'll sit down and give Pastor Hobbs a chance to catch us up on his life. I'll tell you my news first and come back around to explain how it happened."

Carol smiled wide, soaking in the anticipation as Irv ambled to his seat. When he was seated, she burst out, "Y'all, I'm going to write a book!"

"That great!" Pastor Hobbs said. "I've been considering writing Janie Ruth's life story since I told it to all you folks last year. Now, I'll have somebody to motivate me and give me tips."

"I don't know about all that, but you should definitely write your wife's story. If the people in this room are any indication, her story would make an impact in your readers' lives."

"Hey, enough about my book idea. Tell us about yours."

"I'm going to title it *Two of a Kind*, and it's the story of how we came to have two twin black sons and two twin white daughters in the same year. It all started when I got a call from Ebony, Isaiah and Jeremiah's biological mother. Remember, I told y'all last year she wasn't ready to start a relationship with them yet because she had a husband and young children and didn't want to complicate things with them. One day— this would have been back in January or February when I had accompanied Irv to one of his physical therapy appointments—Ebony called.

"She surprised me, but I wondered if she had forgotten to tell me something about the boys' medical history. Instead, she said she and her husband had discussed her setting up an appointment for Isaiah and Jeremiah to meet her if we still approved. I assured her we did, but I wondered what had changed. Turns out, a picture a friend showed their youngest child on his phone forced them to have 'the talk' with him earlier than they had anticipated. Once they did, her husband told her it might be time to tell them about their half-brothers.

"We talked back and forth a few times over the next couple of months while he and Ebony waited for the right opportunity to talk to her children. She called one time to tell me she had put it off long enough, and she wanted me to pray for her before she told her kids. I did, and she asked how to pray for me—I love that she always does that. Well, I told Ebony how nervous I was about caring for Mom, who had come to live with us that week. She suggested waiting to talk to her kids about their older brothers until things settled down with us. Sex is one thing to explain to children, but sexual assault is quite another, especially when it's their mother you're talking about, so she appreciated the reprieve.

"So, time passed and we got so caught up in taking care of Mom that I forgot about Ebony. She called again to check on me in August. I told her Mom seemed to be fading fast. We prayed for each other, and I figured we would end the conversation after that like we usually did. I thanked her for calling, and she didn't respond, so I asked her if she was all right. She didn't answer at first, and I wondered if we had lost our connection, but she said in a quiet little voice, 'Carol, I told 'em.' I needed her to repeat it, but I understood what she meant. She told me not to rush, but she was ready.

"About a week after Mom died, Irv and I were enjoying our morning coffee on the deck out back. The girls had leased an apartment in August but put off moving into it until Mom passed. They were excited to have their own place after living at home their entire lives. After the funeral I didn't want to hold them back any longer, so I told them to please pack their stuff and go enjoy their new place. They were still coming by and getting some of their clothes and other things throughout the week, but with Mom gone and them, too, the house seemed incredibly empty.

"Anyway, we had started on our second cups when I recalled my last conversation with Ebony. Irv must have thought me crazy because I jumped up and said, 'I need to call!' I abandoned him on the deck without telling him about my epiphany. I called Ebony to see if she and her husband wanted to come over during the weekend and talk through the best way to reintroduce her to Isaiah and Jeremiah. Poor Irv. I walked back outside talking ninety to nothing, and he had no idea what I was yakking about.

"Two things happened that weekend that led me to the book. I'm no writer by any stretch of the imagination. I mean, I did well in English classes in school, but I understand that some stories we write, and some stories we live. Once we've lived them, it sure makes the writing part easier. Darrius—that's Ebony's husband—told me that. She was so eager to meet that they dropped by for lunch later the same day. We caught the husbands up to speed on our phone conversation and let Darrius get to know us and Irv get to know them. We couldn't set a time for the introductions until we conferred with Isaiah and Jeremiah, but we handled much of the preliminary work.

"With all that covered, Darrius looked back and forth between Ebony and me and told us our story would make an interesting book. He had just finished reading a book, a true story about a rich white man who befriended a homeless black man. He said our story would be as interesting as theirs, what with all of our mixed family experiences. Ebony said she didn't want to share the story of how the twins were conceived, but that we should consider what Darrius said.

"I didn't have too much time to consider it then because Irv had bought us tickets to a marriage conference at our church that started late that afternoon. As soon as Darrius and Ebony left, we rushed to get ready for the conference, which was exceptional, exactly what Irv and I needed. The couple who led it had written two books that were part of our registration packet, and we stood in line afterward to get them to sign our copies. We were re-connecting with some old friends, catching them up on why they hadn't seen much of us, so we ended up at the very back of the line. After our long day, we considered skipping the signing at that point to go home and straight to bed.

"I wanted to speak to authors of the books, though. Writing a book had dominated my thoughts during every spare moment of the conference, and here were two people who had written several. I didn't know anybody else who had written a book, so we waited. When we finally reached the front of the line, I could tell they were relieved to see us. Again, I thought about just letting them sign the book and go on to their hotel to get some rest. I couldn't do it, though."

25

"Hi, I'm Carol Turner, and this is my husband, Irv."

"James and Jeanette Varnado," the husband said, extending his hand to shake Irv's. "Thanks for coming to the conference tonight."

"Guess you're glad to see us?" James responded to Carol's question with a quizzical look. "End of the line."

"Oh, right. I hope it's not that obvious. We are introverts by nature. We love doing this, but it drains us. When people tell us their stories as we sign books, though, it lets us know what we're doing is worth the effort."

"Do you mind one more story and perhaps a question or two about writing? I'm sorry, it might take a few minutes, but today has been a trying day for us, too. We waited until last so we could ask you for some direction about what I feel like the Lord is leading me to do."

James glanced at Jeanette, who nodded. "Tell you what—Carol and Irv, right? Our team is almost finished packing our gear. Could we possibly take this conversation to an ice cream shop? We usually wind down after doing one of these single-night conferences over a milkshake. If you'd like to join us, that would give your story a chance to breathe a little. We noticed a place near the hotel where we're staying called Gold Zone Sweets. Are you familiar with it?"

"Oh, yeah," Irv answered. "Everybody around here knows Gold Zone. If there's a particular flavor you like —or even a combination of flavors—they'll have it, and it'll be good, too."

"Great. Give us ten minutes to finish up here, and we'll meet you there."

Twenty minutes later, James and Jeanette joined Irv and Carol inside a still-crowded Gold Zone Sweets. When the four received their orders, they took a seat and spent a minute going around the table to compare flavors. Jeanette invited Carol to share what was on her heart. She shared a little background, slowed down with their adoption and birth of two sets of twins, and fast-forwarded to their recent care of Carol's mother.

"That's a fascinating story," Jeanette said. "So this is the book you feel the Lord is leading you to write? Irv, are you on board? Writing a book is a major commitment."

"Yes," Irv said. "And our daughters moved out this week. I assumed it would be such a relief to get a little peace and quiet, but we went straight from chaos to lonely. It was like you guys said tonight, married couples need vision and purpose. We had plenty of that, for sure, but it's like our journey as parents and as children ourselves ended in the same week. Carol's mom was the last living parent for either of us, and our boy twins are both married and gone. But today, we jumped right back into excitement and vision and purpose. I'll let Carol tell you about that."

"Are you guys okay with listening for a little while longer?" Carol asked.

James was in the middle of a deep swallow of strawberry-mango-pineapple milkshake, so he lifted his index finger from his straw to bid her go on. Carol told about connecting with the boy twins' mother and how they had decided just that day to set up a meeting between her and her biological sons. "Almost as a side note, her husband said something about my writing a book about my experiences, especially the story of boy black twins and girl white twins growing up in the same house. I'm not someone who has always wanted to write a book, but I'm telling you, the idea won't leave me alone. I don't even know where to start, but I'm excited to get started. I realize you probably have people asking you about writing and speaking all the time, but if you guys could point me in a direction, I will figure out the rest."

Jeanette said, "I can tell you we had a lot of help. Neither of us would have considered ourselves writers, either, but I guess once you've published a book or two, the label fits. I have learned there are many ways to publish nowadays. It's all a matter of what you want to accomplish with your book. For us, it's not so much about selling books as it is having a business card, you might say, for our conferences. James and I are hardly role models for the perfect marriage, but the Lord has given us a story to tell. Churches and other groups are more likely to pay us to speak if we have a book we can point them to so they can read what we are going to present. We add a little to the cost for someone to attend our conference so we can include our books as a refresher that will help people on down the road. We're not in this for the money, but we need it to pay the bills if we're to keep doing this full time. Do you know your purpose?"

"Not really, but people find our story interesting and unique. I'm not opposed to telling it if everyone involved gives me the go ahead, especially if it would bring somebody else some help or encouragement in their journey. But I don't have any formal training as a writer.

"Tell you what," James said, "give me your email address, and I'll send you a list of all the people we use. We publish our own materials, but we contract with cover designers, editors, and graphic designers for some of our promotional stuff. It's all in one file with phone numbers, email addresses, prices, and all that. I'd be glad to send it to you. As far as the writing goes, everybody kind of has his own style. I would say get started and hire an editor with whom you're comfortable to do an overall assessment of your work. A good editor can steer you in the right direction before you get too far along. I guarantee you plenty of editors will want to work with your story."

"That would be so helpful, James. Thank you. Do you mind if I ask your opinion about one more thing?"

James slurped the last of his milkshake. "Shoot."

"Maybe it's weird, but I already have a title in mind. It's been rolling around in my head all day. We've told you the gist of our story. How does *Two of a Kind* sound?"

"Hmm," James answered, cocking his head to the side and staring into space. "*Two of a Kind... Two of a Kind*—initial impression? Reminds me of a country music song. *We're two of a kind, working on a full...* wait, that's it! With your new season of life, why don't you title it *Two of a Kind: Working on an Empty House*?"

"I. Love. It. Irv, what do you think?"

"I'd buy it."

"Jeanette?"

"I'd buy it. We'll make you a deal. You write your book, and we'll write the foreword for you if you'd like."

Carol squealed and clapped her hands, drawing the attention of other patrons. "You've got a deal."

"SO I'VE BEEN WRITING a book. The learning curve has been steep, but I have plenty of time. I decided not to return to work until next spring, so I want to maximize my time between now and then. I write for three hours first thing in the morning and try to watch a video or read a book about writing before lunch. I spend a couple more hours in the afternoon either writing or planning. Every evening, I try to talk to someone involved in our story to get his or her perspective about whatever part of our story I'm working. If you look at the hours it's taking, I'm working a full-time job plus overtime, but I am loving every minute.

"Earlier this month, I sent the first part of our story to five different editors from the list James and Jeanette Varnado sent us and to a few agents. I started with our desire to have a baby and how that worked itself out for us. Four of the five editors responded within a week and wanted to work with me. One lady—she was so sweet—said that if she didn't have any bills to pay, she would help me publish our story for free. I heard from two agents who told me they thought they could get me a book deal with a publisher, so we have some options."

"What kind of feedback did you receive?" asked Pastor Hobbs.

"To sum up what was most consistent in their reviews, I get lost in the weeds sometimes, telling too many details instead of moving the story along. On the positive side, every single one of them believed it was a story worth sharing, and they thought it would sell if I took the time to do it right. They all liked the title, too."

"If you need any early readers, please include us. Also, once you have a publication date, I want to reserve you and Irv to come tell your story at my church."

"Same here," Easton said. "Sherill and I could make that happen at our church."

"We want you to come to ours, too," Tara said. "Don't we, Pops?"

"Sure do. Carol, don't waste time because I'm not going to live forever."

CAROL TOOK A DEEP, satisfying breath. She knew she needed to wrap up her part of the unscripted program, but telling the story of her year had been therapeutic. Pastor Hobbs asked if he she minded his taking a photo of her family. He had brought his camera in case there were opportunities for pictures, and this seemed like as a perfect time. Carol leaped like a schoolgirl and called Irv, her daughters, and her sons and their wives forward. The seats at the back two tables emptied, save for the boyfriends'.

The family lined up quickly, each taking their customary position in the family photo. Irv moved to Carol's left, flanked by Beth, Isaiah, and Aliyah. Kate stood by her mother with Jeremiah and Rebecca down the line. With everyone set, Pastor Hobbs counted, "One, two…"

"I wish I could be in the picture," Garen blurted. "You?"

Michael nodded. "It's a family photo, though. I get it."

When they saw eyeballs turning in their direction, Garen said, "Too loud?"

"Obviously."

"I still want in, don't you?"

"Yes. Where do you reckon they would put us?"

"Beside the girls, obviously."

"Makes sense. You ready?"

"Yep."

As the boys walked to the front to hijack the family picture, Carol leaned over and whispered in Irv's ear,

"Just let them. Don't make a big deal about it. We can take another one later if you want."

Irv whispered back, "I think you'll be satisfied with this one."

When Garen and Michael reached the front, they asked Irv, "Where do you want us?" Both of them stood in front of Irv with their hands in their pockets. Their flippant manner grated on Carol's nerves, as she had not known either of them to act like this. *Must be me. Irv doesn't seem to be bothered.*

"Garen, you stand in front of Beth," Irv said, "and Michael, you go stand in front of Kate." The young men complied.

"In front of them?" Carol started, but her question turned to a shriek when Garen and Michael turned, dropped to a knee, and held up rings. Carol slapped Irv on the arm. "You knew about this, didn't you?"

"You didn't imagine a young man would ask one of our daughters to marry him without asking for my blessing first, did you?"

"No, but... when?"

"They both came to me while your mother was still with us, and they were far more classy than you gave them credit for just now. They figured tonight was as fine a time as any to surprise the girls. The picture was a setup."

Carol spun around. "Pastor, you were in on this, too?"

"Playing my role, Ms. Carol," Pastor Hobbs said with a shrug. "Now, that family photo?"

"Oh, yes, yes. Guys, why don't you stand kind of behind and between the girls and their brothers?"

"Uh, Mom?" Kate asked.

"Yes?"

"You didn't give us a chance to answer."

"Answer what?"

"Uh…"

"Oh, my gosh, I'm so sorry! This night has just been too much! By all means, go ahead." Kate and Beth answered by pulling Michael and Garen into their places for the first family photo of many they hoped to take.

"All right, let's try this again," Pastor Hobbs said. "One… two… three!" He clicked his camera while the rest of the crowd captured the moment on their phones.

Amid the photos of smaller groups that followed, Carol pressed her face close to Irv's. "Even with your rehab and everything that happened with Mom, this has been the best year of my life. Think about it, honey: I became a 5K winner, grandmother, bride, empty nester, author, speaker, and now mother of the bride times two. It's almost too much for one person to take in a year's time."

Irv kissed her gently on the lips. "Then I'm glad I stuck around to walk through it with you."

CALVIN

26

"What a night," Pastor Hobbs started. "Austen, I want to say thank you again for showing a little kindness to some lonely-looking strangers last year. I'm sure you didn't realize it would produce such a litany of inspirational stories, but then again, you never know what the ripple effect of a good deed might be. And Laticia, you did amazing job coordinating everything with Austen and the rest of us. I don't mean to beat it to death, but let's not miss the lesson of a season of loneliness being cured by a simple act of altruism."

"Preach it, Pastor!" yelled Pops.

Calvin grinned. "Forgive me—I've been doing it so long I slip right into it sometimes. The fact is, I felt as lonely as I ever have when I walked through the doors of The Log Cabin last year. That's not a familiar emotion for me because I always had Janie Ruth to prop me back up when I was down. When she wasn't here all of a sudden, the people in my church tried their best, but they weren't Janie Ruth. I felt right sorry for myself when I ate my Thanksgiving meal all alone last year.

"What a difference a few minutes makes. I transitioned from being downcast one minute, then to noticed, then to part of a community of like-minded people, even though we came from all different walks of life. What a difference *a year* makes. Can you believe it? I'm reminded of my favorite movie, *It's a Wonderful Life*, when George Bailey gets to see what the world might have been like if he had never been born. It's easy to imagine where loneliness, bitterness, purposelessness, and addiction may have pushed some of us, if not all of us. Instead, we created a group of people who care for one another, who inspire and encourage one another, and who count on one another.

"After we met last Thanksgiving, I purposed to pour into other people so my focus wouldn't be on me. That's never been who I am. I have appreciated being able to invest in some of your lives this year. I don't take lightly the weight of the mistakes and regrets you carried for years until you trusted me with them.

"Yours weren't the only weighty matters with which I have dealt with this year. In February my friend Roger Stapleford stunned our entire congregation when he announced he had Stage IV liver cancer. He said it so casually during one of our home group Bible studies that it didn't register at first. Remember, I told you guys about Roger last year. He and Vicki welcomed Janie Ruth and me here after Katrina. He put me to work repairing roofs so I could afford to preach and lead our church. Roger was the financial muscle behind the West

Cary Miracle, the programs Janie Ruth started at the school that is changing so many lives there. Roger didn't just write checks, though; he showed up week after week to serve those kids in person. Most men of Roger's standing would have claimed they were too busy, but not him. He intentionally built into people in his construction business, too, to allow himself the freedom to serve outside the company.

"It was such a shock to hear Roger say he had just a few weeks left to live—surreal, really. I wanted to fight in prayer, but Roger told us to save our prayers for Vicki and their two sons, who would speed up their transition into leadership with his company. God had given him a peace about his home going. He called his last few weeks a victory lap. Roger died four weeks to the day after he told us he had cancer. We saw him shrink from a healthy two hundred pounds to a buck-fifty, but the closer he walked toward home, the more his countenance reflected the godly man he was.

"On the day before I had to preach my wife's funeral, when I didn't know if I had the wherewithal to do it, we talked for a long while. Roger volunteered to be strong on my behalf. He made me promise that whenever I sensed I was ready to cave under the grief, I would find him in the audience for strength. When I stood up before our family and loved ones and took a breath to say my first words, the first wave threatened to take me down in the pulpit. I remembered to look at Roger, though, and he held his fist right below his smile that told me I could do it for my precious wife's memory. I counted on his strength—God's strength through him—several times during the message, but I made it through. The importance of making it through was that I shared the gospel at the end of my message. Five of Janie Ruth's former students at West Cary gave their lives to Jesus that day. It was amazing.

"Roger stayed back at the church to assist those five new believers begin their new walks with Christ. He missed the graveside service of a great friend to help those young people, and I'll never forget what he said to me afterward. 'Calvin,' he said, 'Your pastor friend was going to do the graveside service. If you fell apart then, it would be okay. But nothing I could do would honor Janie Ruth more than helping those precious young people she loved so much learn to walk with the King.

"After the graveside service, I drove by the church to find Roger kneeling at an altar in the front of the sanctuary. I wanted to thank him for staying, but when he raised his head to see who was walking up behind him, any strength I still had vanished. I fell to my knees at the altar and just wept and wept and wept. Roger didn't say a word. He was just there, and I trusted him to stay with me until the biggest wave of grief washed ashore.

"I don't remember how long it took—fifteen or twenty minutes, maybe—but my eyes eventually cried themselves dry. I wiped the altar and staggered to my feet. When Roger wrapped his arms around me, it restored my will to face people again. He looked me dead in the eye and told me today was temporary, but those young people giving their lives to Jesus proved we both still had kingdom work to do. I said, 'Let's get started,' and we left."

Vicki Stapleford nodded and smiled at Pastor Hobbs, who daubed his eyes with a tissue as she curled her fist beneath her chin.

"Many times over the last weeks of Roger's life," Pastor Hobbs continued. "I would catch his eye and raise my fist in front of my chin to remind him he could count on me for strength as I had depended on him. He would smile and keep going. His victory lap was nothing short of a celebration of his life's work. I'm not talking about construction, either; that was just his work the Lord blessed so he could give like nobody I've ever known. He made his rounds in those last weeks to write one more check to the organizations he supported and tell *them* how much they had blessed *him*. He set up a foundation Vicki and his sons will run so his legacy doesn't end with his ability to write a check.

"Roger wanted me to take his victory lap with him. He asked how much I made at my other job. When I told him, he wrote me a check for three months' pay and worked it out with my boss for me to make the circuit with him. We visited three mission organizations, a women's shelter, a halfway house, two high schools and a college, the homeless shelter where Janie Ruth and I served, a construction ministry, a disaster relief ministry, and a seminary. The ultimate stop on his list—because he wanted to save his favorite for last—was West Cary. He scheduled meetings with the principals from all three schools and wrote a check for Janie Ruth's programs at the elementary school to continue for quite some time. He gifted the middle school a new learning center decked out with the latest technology. He told the principal at the high school he wanted to set up a scholarship fund in Janie Ruth's name, but he discovered Mr. Jimmy Lee had beaten him to it."

Pops grinned. "I don't win too many races nowadays."

"Well, I used Roger's slight hesitation after hearing that to suggest to the principal that he use Roger's gift to set up the Roger and Vicki Stapleford scholarship fund. Roger protested, but the principal ran with it. He told Roger he wanted his school's legacy to be that they gave to help their fellow man. If what they had was time and ideas, give them. If what they had was financial resources, give them. What better way than to present scholarships to remind West Cary students they had been the beneficiary of both types of giving. The four of us wore Roger down—not that he had much might remaining—and he gave in to a scholarship fund in his and Vicki's names. Between Mr. Jimmy Lee's and Roger's endowments, every kid who graduates from West Cary High School will get some help going to college from now on.

"It was one of the greatest blessings of my life to accompany Roger on his victory lap. He talked to the folks at West Cary on a Tuesday, and that was it. After spending a few days making sure he finished well with Vicki, he passed away the following weekend. I find there are times I want to tell him something, and I have to remind myself he's not there. I took some widower lessons from Mr. Jimmy Lee, though, so I learned to go to the places special to Roger and me and talk to him like he was there. Pops is right: If you've been close enough to someone, you realize what they're going to say.

"One day, I told Vicki about what I'd learned from Mr. Jimmy Lee, and she thought she might like to give it a try. The next week was the week before the kids came back to school, so I drove over to West Cary to walk the halls and say hello to the teachers and encourage them. I asked Vicki to go, and it was a tough time because we dealt with our losses again and again as we visited with each teacher. But we enjoyed going back to where Janie Ruth and Roger continue to make such an impact.

"When the teachers left for the day, we crossed the road to a hamburger stand to grab something to eat. We took our bags of food back across to the picnic table in the shady area beside the school. On one of the few school days I could help out, Roger and I would some-times eat a burger and drink a sweet tea there while Janie Ruth and Vicki worked with the kids in the after-school program. When we sat down there in August, I imagined Roger sitting there and told him about our day. Vicki remained unsure at first, but she joined in after a while. We didn't stay more than ten or fifteen minutes, just enough to pass on the wonderful things the teachers said about him. You can linger too long, Mr. Jimmy Lee taught me, so I drove Vicki home. She didn't talk much on the way home, but I could tell she was holding back tears. When we reached her house, she said, 'Please tell Mr. Jimmy Lee thank you for me.'"

27

"Two weeks later, I stopped by the dollar store on the way home to pick up a few things, and I ran into Vicki. It was the first time I had seen her since our conversation with Roger, except from a distance at church. She seemed a little nervous, so I asked her why."

"Calvin, I can't tell you how much it meant to me to sit in the grove at the school and talk to Roger. Your friend was right—I could almost hear him talking back to me, and that bothers me. I've been talking to Roger around the house and 'hearing' him respond, but—I don't know—is it a little strange to be speaking and listening to the dead? I'm pretty sure I caught the cat staring at me yesterday, but you still seem normal enough."

Calvin smiled and reached out to touch Vicki on the

arm. "I'm glad I'm not the only one who wrestles with that. When Mr. Jimmy Lee told our group about talking to his dead wife and his dead best friend and his dead mother last year, I was a little spooked, too. He came across as genuine, though, so I gave him the benefit of the doubt, at least until I talked to him about it. During my years in the ministry, I have seen plenty of people who genuinely believed in something far from truth, so I was still plenty skeptical. I mean, I pastored in New Orleans, so I've seen my share of people who were genuine—genuinely off their rockers. Pops—I mean, Mr. Jimmy Lee—didn't strike me as one of those people.

"I asked to go with him sometime, wondering if our conversation about talking to dead loved ones would end there. Instead, he invited me to come along the next day. He did that thing he does—tells you not to wait too long because he's ninety-three years old—so I met him at the church cemetery where his friend Jeremiah is buried. I arrived first because I wanted to walk around and get a sense of the history of the church's people, but I found the gate locked. Pops pulled up a few minutes later, and I informed him of our slight dilemma. He laughed and pulled out a key.

"I brought a chair, like he told me to do. We sat down and this very pleasant but spunky old man started talking. He introduced me to his best friend Jeremiah and told me how they had met. He would say things like, 'You remember, Jeremiah? Oh, sure, I'll take him out to the place we met—maybe next time.' The entire thirty minutes we sat in the cemetery, ours seemed like a natural conversation among three friends.

Mr. Jimmy Lee even warned Jeremiah I might be a little skeptical, but it would be okay. He told his friend I had suffered a daunting loss in my life and he was teaching me how he coped with losing his best friend. He told Jeremiah he wouldn't press me to say anything and continued talking to him. I'll tell you, Vicki, I almost told my story to a dead man I had never met."

"What kept you from sharing it?"

"As natural as it felt, it still seemed like… the best comparison I can make is going to an awe-inspiring musical. Even though you realize you're suspending reality to enter the world of the play, you get so caught up in the story and the music, it almost seems real. When the action pauses for intermission, you mill around the lobby with other people as captivated and involved in the story as you are. After the play is over and the actors and actresses stand in the back of the lobby, audience members talk to them like they are personally acquainted with them. On a certain level, they are. But they engaged with the character, not the actor. Later, when you go out for dessert, the play becomes less real, and you can't convey the deep emotional place the story affected you to someone who wasn't there. To someone in the audience who 'got it' like you did, words aren't necessary. Does that make sense?"

"Perfect. Roger and I had season tickets to the community theater, and certain plays—especially musicals—overwhelmed both of us. We saw some duds along the way, but the superb ones—they reached a part deep in your soul that you didn't even recognize existed. Good art always inspired the generous side of Roger."

"Okay, that's how the day with Mr. Jimmy Lee seemed to me. It seemed real enough—and at some level it was—but something in my mind kept reminding me what we were doing. Afterward, when we stood in the parking lot next to our vehicles, he asked me if I had questions. I had an important one. 'Mr. Jimmy Lee, when you're talking to Jeremiah, do you... does he... speak back to you?'

"I'm sure he got a little put out with me, but he responded with a series of questions. 'Calvin, do you spend time with the Lord in the morning most days?' I said yes. 'Do you ever journal?' I told him I had mountains of journals I had written in over the years. 'Have you ever listened to an audiobook or a podcast?' I said I considered them entertaining company on the drive back and forth to work each day. 'Calvin, do you consider audiobooks actual books?' I wasn't picking up on his line of reasoning at all, but I said sure, they have the same content. Then, he asked if I would consider him weird if he kept a journal or even wrote a book about his memories of Jeremiah or his wife or his mother. I began to understand where he was leading. I told him no, that plenty of people had written books in that manner. 'And would it be weird to listen to a book like that rather than read it?' No, I told him, it wouldn't. He smiled, proud of himself for phrasing it so I could understand. He wasn't finished, though."

"What else did he say?"

"He said, 'Calvin, to be sure, Jeremiah's voice is clear

in my head, but it's not him speaking from the dead. He doesn't tell me to do crazy things. The only reason his voice and Catherine's and Mama's are still strong to me is because I've made this a practice for so long. A single old codger spending as much time alone as I do can become self-absorbed if his is the only voice he ever hears talking back to him. Sometimes, I need to think in voices of people who tell me the truth and don't sugar-coat it. If that's weird, count me slap goofy. You wouldn't be the first person to accuse me of being a few degrees off dead center. I figure Janie Ruth told you plenty you needed to hear about yourself but didn't want to say. There may be times hearing yourself think through her voice will work for you, too. If you find it doesn't work for you, don't do it, simple as that.'"

"That makes sense. Did y'all leave it there?"

"Yes. I 'took Janie Ruth out to eat' that night at Peas and Butterbeans, which is where we often visited when we had something we needed to talk about. It's where Janie Ruth first told me about her vision for what would become the West Cary Miracle."

Vicki's face brightened with a far-off smile. "Oh, yes, Roger and I had some great times and important talks with y'all at Peas and Butterbeans, too. If you'll remember, she laid out the West Cary project to Roger and me there, too."

"Yeah, I had forgotten it was there. Well, I asked for our usual table in the back corner, kind of away from the crowd. I ordered…"

"… country fried steak with mashed potatoes and gravy, purple hull peas, and fried okra because you can't even stand the smell of the turnip greens Janie Ruth always ordered."

"You remember?"

"Y'all were so cute, always ordering alike except your okra and her turnip greens. Most places we ate, you would order the same thing every time."

"Guilty. You tell me the restaurant where we're eating, you've decided what I'm going to eat, for sure. Neither Janie Ruth nor I ventured far away from something we liked at a particular restaurant. Anyway, I sat down at our usual table for the first time without her, and ordered my usual, except I added sweet tea with lemon. Trust me, she scolded me for ordering an overpriced drink. I told her to hush—I had no sweet tea at home because she wasn't there, and I hadn't gotten around to making another pitcher. I didn't say that out loud, but her presence seemed almost as real.

"While I sat eating in silence to the outside world, I had a long conversation with Janie Ruth about my intentions to make a practice of going to our favorite places and talking to her. She let me do most of the talking, but at the end, when I was eating my peach cobbler, her voice was strong, like she was sitting across from me. Vicki, she said, 'Now, Calvin, I'm all for your not forgetting any of what we built together for the glory of God, but I also want you to remember He took me, not you. You have better days to live, more kingdom work to accomplish. Don't forget me, but you live your life.' She repeated it for double emphasis."

"Oh, that is *so* Janie Ruth," Vicki said, a little too loud for the discount store. Lowering her voice, she continued, "If she ever had anything important to say, she always said it twice. You better pay attention, Calvin."

"Trust me, I am."

"But talking to her in your mind didn't feel peculiar?"

"Only a little. And less with practice. Do you consider me an odd bird?"

"No, Calvin, you're unique among people in this world, but in the best of ways."

"Okay, after visiting with Roger that day before school started, I figured you might have been weirded out."

"Not really. I still have one reservation, though."

"Shoot."

"Well, how can you tell when you're living in the past? I realize how terrible that sounds with Roger being gone only a few months. When he was down to his last few days—after his victory lap—he talked to the boys one day about their roles as dads to his grandchildren and leaders of the family business. Mostly, though, when he was awake, we talked, just the two of us. We reminisced about the key moments of our life together and talked about how the struggles made us more resilient and more attune to needs around us. On the last day he wasn't overcome by pain medication, we talked about my life after him, even though the topic was one I had tried to avoid. He wanted me to make sure I worked through grief properly, told me you understood how to do it better than anybody he knew, and to lean on you.

"Near the end of our talk that day, Roger told me he never wanted me to wonder about one thing in particular, and then he released me to marry again. He said it might happen soon or years later, but I didn't owe him anything other than to grieve properly so I could let him go. He assured me he had prepared our sons for another man in my life. Calvin, I didn't like his talking like that—didn't even want to think about it—but he insisted. I'm glad he did. The thing is, I'm still hurting over losing Roger, but the joy of what we had outweighs the sorrow most days. I'm afraid if I keep 'meeting' with him, I'll try to hold on to something I should let go. Does that make sense?"

"It sure does. Although Janie Ruth didn't realize she was going to die the day she did, we talked sometimes about what we wanted for the other if God called one of us home before the other. We agreed we desired each other to feel no obligations except loving each other most."

Vicki smiled. "Yeah, we said something like that, too. Anyway, I understand how talking to Janie Ruth has helped you, but I wanted to mention another perspective."

"Thank you, I'll sure spend some time pondering it. I saw how well it worked for Mr. Jimmy Lee and how much peace he has and figured I'd give it a shot. Remember, he said what worked for him might not work for me."

"But didn't you say it was working for you? I had no intention of talking you out of anything."

"Yes, but I didn't tell you how my conversations

with Janie Ruth always seem to end."

"Do tell."

"I keep sensing she's telling me to let her go. I don't want to listen to her because I don't want to dishonor her. Every time I imagine us talking, though, she tells me her race is over and mine has some time left. If I don't get to it, I might miss out on how the Lord wants to use however many days I have left before I join her. There, I've said it out loud. I haven't wanted to, and pastors can sometimes find it hard to say difficult things to anybody else, even other pastors. We don't really have our act together as much as people assume we do."

"Calvin, after all these years and all our families have been through together, you can tell me anything, and I'll understand."

"Thanks. When I looked at my schedule this morning, I didn't have a 5:30 counseling appointment at the dollar store on my calendar."

"I'll send you a bill."

"I'd pay it."

"Oh, you know better. Let's talk soon."

"Okay, see you at church Sunday."

"Seen you Sunday." Vicki started forward, stopped, and then wrapped her arms around Pastor Hobbs's neck for a quick hug. He placed one hand on her shoulder and gave it a pat. She wished Calvin a wonderful week and walked through the door a moment later. He lingered until she pulled out of her parking spot, enjoying the flowery aroma of her perfume on his collar. When she pulled away, he picked up a can of chili and a box of saltines and rushed home to cook supper.

28

"Mr. Jimmy Lee, I don't mean to cast any dispersions on your practice of talking to your loved ones," Pastor Hobbs said. "It works for you and you're a fine, levelheaded man."

"You don't have to tiptoe through the tulips with me, Pastor. I'll do me and you do you, and we'll get along just fine. Matter of fact, when I told Catherine I had told you about trying to pretend to spend some time with your wife, you know what she said?"

"No, tell me."

"She said you would think I was off my rocker. Truth be told, I might be a few bricks shy of a load, but aren't we all?"

"Yes, sir, I suppose so. I'll tell you one thing: I don't seek conversations with Janie Ruth, but I hear her voice and imagine what she would say about so many things. I realize that might fade, but I think she would want it to. She was a different sort like that. That's one thing I loved most about her, still love most about her."

Paula Gull broke in. "So what's… this?" she asked, extending her hands and turning back and forth between Pastor Hobbs where Vicki Stapleford sat.

"Yes, Paula, never one to beat around the bush, are you?"

"Not really. So what gives?"

"It's a long story, but here goes. Do you remember the tornadoes that went through this area one early afternoon back in the middle of May?"

"Sure, we were watching it and ready to go to our safe place when it changed directions and missed town."

"Yes, well, it may have missed town, but it didn't just disappear. When it changed directions, it headed toward the country where I live and where my church is located. We had eleven minutes after it changed directions before the weatherman said it would hit us. As soon as I saw that on TV, I called my deacons to get the word out so everybody would get to safety. There aren't but forty families in our church, so each deacon calls their folks to check on them and to get out the word when something unusual happens.

"Once I got ahold of my deacons, I started calling around to my neighbors who aren't church members to make sure they were moving somewhere safe. Amongst those phone calls, Vicki called and told me I best be getting on over to their house where I'd be safer than at my house. Roger, being in construction and all, had built a good-sized safe room in their house. Plus, he had told me our little house wouldn't be much of a match for the tornadoes that often come through that area. Katrina had been enough of a storm to last Janie Ruth and me a lifetime, so we took him up on the offer during serious storms. This was the first one since she and Roger passed."

VICKI'S FRAZZLED VOICE ASKED, "Calvin, are you still at home?"

"I've been calling church members and neighbors. They may not have seen that the storm changed course and is heading toward us."

"We've got six minutes, and it'll take you four to get here. You better hurry!"

"Vicki, I didn't... with Roger... I..."

"Calvin, quit your stammering and get over here! You remember what Roger always said about that house of yours. Now, start driving!"

Pastor Hobbs grabbed his keys, his rain jacket, and his Bible and ran out the door. Four minutes later, he screeched to a stop in the circle drive in front of the Staplefords' house. The rumble of the storm met him when he opened his door. A quick glance at the southwestern sky and he saw the funnel cloud forming.

Vicki stood at the open front door, waving frantically. "Calvin, get in here!"

Together they ran through the house and into the safe room.

"Are you crazy?" she asked. "That storm's headed right toward us. Didn't you hear the rumbling?"

"Yeah. I just had to make sure I called everybody on my list."

"Calvin, that's a cell phone in your hand. It moves. You could have called everybody on your way here."

"I guess that's true. When I saw it change direction, though, all I thought about was alerting everybody around me."

Vicki closed the door behind them. "Are you sure that's all?"

"What do you mean?"

"You weren't coming, were you, Calvin? Tell me the truth."

He had avoided revealing his motive as long as he could. "No, Vicki, I planned to hunker down in the bathroom in the hall. I didn't want to impose."

"Impose?!? It's a tornado, for crying out loud. There's no telling what damage it's causing outside right now. It might destroy your house, and you were afraid to impose?"

"Vicki, I'll be honest with you, I don't feel comfortable here with just the two of us. Our church members have been very understanding and supportive of both of us, but I don't want them to get the wrong idea."

"The wrong idea about what?"

"About us."

"And what idea would they be getting? We haven't done anything wrong."

"No, of course we haven't. I'm not implying that.

But I just want to make sure that I—that we—stay above reproach."

"And haven't we?"

"Yes, but…"

"Calvin, it's not right!" Vicki seemed almost angry. "We're longtime friends who have suffered loss, and we can't lean on each other because of what people might think?"

Calvin forced a smile. "I'm not sure I'm comfortable having this conversation in a windowless storm shelter of the widow of one of my best friends."

Vicki's countenance lightened a little, but not for long. "Fine, the storm has passed by now. Let's go outside where the universe can watch two friends protecting ourselves from a tornado and pass judgment."

Calvin couldn't flee the storm shelter fast enough. His concern for what was going on with Vicki outweighed his own discomfort, but he felt ready to suffocate. As soon as they stepped into the hall of Vicki's house, though, his phone buzzed.

Hey, Pastor Hobbs, I hope the tornado didn't hit you there as hard as it hit us here. Thank God we had no deaths or major injuries, but the school has taken a lot of damage. Sure would appreciate help with cleanup and maybe some meals for the workers that are already showing up if you can arrange it. Please let me know as soon as you can.

"What is it?" Vicki asked, her frustration giving over to concern.

"Principal at West Cary High School. Tornado did some damage to the school, and, I'm sure, the houses nearby. He's asking for help as soon as we can get it to him."

"I'll call my sons and get them to send over some equipment. The food trailer is out back. I'll hook it up to Roger's truck and drive it over."

"Great. I'll call the deacons and get them to get all the folks on the disaster relief team mobilized. I'm going home to get my chain saw and gas cans." Looking around and seeing several sizable limbs on the ground but little more, Pastor Hobbs said, "I just hope my house is still there."

"Okay, see you there. Oh, don't forget to text him back that we'll be there."

Pastor Hobbs saw a few trees down alongside the road but little other damage between Vicki's house and his. By the time he drove the three miles home, he had notified the disaster relief team of the need and set a plan in motion. His cottage-style house was missing a few shingles but otherwise unharmed. He grabbed his chainsaw, gas cans, big bottle of bar and chain oil, and three ten-packs of work gloves and threw them in the back of his S-10. Before heading to West Cary twenty minutes away, he stopped by the church to unlock it for the cooking team to grab the foodstuffs they kept on hand in the church kitchen.

Both the chainsaw team and cooking team had seen duty from Florida to Texas and many points in between. Their disaster relief squad joined others who did everything from housing to mud out to counseling in the wake of major storms and was well regarded in that arena. The chainsaw team—made of of two dozen men, some church members and some neighbors—arrived first at West Cary High School, where the bulk of the damage had occurred. After a quick tour from the assistant principal on the scene, Pastor Hobbs and his team prioritized their work and prepared their chainsaws for action. The food truck turned into the school parking lot about the time the first wood chips flew.

CALVIN HOBBS HAD ALWAYS KNOWN hard work for people in need. He had rebuilt barns, repaired fences, rebuilt engines, plowed fields, and much more. When farmers in his community found themselves in a pinch, they could always count on him to help. He loved it when a farmer offered to pay him, and he told them no. They would insist, "Aw, Pastor, I wasn't expecting you to work for free." He would respond, "Tell you what, when you come to church on Sunday, just put it in the plate. The Lord can multiply it better than I can." They would, and the church continued to serve in ways much larger churches envied. In addition, the pastor and his wife always had plenty of fruits, vegetables, and meat to last through every winter, too.

THE CHAINSAWS RAN out of gas one after another about an hour into the crew's work. The group convened for a break and a bottle of water. Many of the locals that Pastor Hobbs knew from Janie Ruth's programs walked over with their plates of spaghetti and asked if they could prepare plates for the men.

"We're going to go through one more tankful before we stop," Pastor Hobbs answered. "Tell you what, though, why don't you guys stick around after you finish and make a list of other places where we can come back throughout the week and help. We'll get it from you and chat for a bit when we take our supper break."

By the time their tanks ran dry again, the men had cut the trees away from the school building and taken down two smaller trees leaning precariously close to the front awning. The sun had dropped low in the sky, and the younger guys in their crew suggested they keep working until dark.

"We'd all be better served to take a break and eat something," Pastor Hobbs said, "especially us older fellows." It was a running joke among the team that one of the younger men would suggest they keep going when they needed a break. One of the older men who worked circles around them would feign a need to stop. "Let's get something to eat before they shut down the catering service."

THE MEN JOINED the locals waiting in line for spaghetti, peas, corn, rolls, and sweet tea. The team of four men and twelve women had the food service side of the relief effort well under control. Vicki dished heaping portions of spaghetti on the plates of the chainsaw team. She was all smiles and in her element. The men didn't wait long before grabbing seats in metal chairs marked "Property of West Cary High School" at folding tables pulled from the school cafeteria. Pastor Hobbs sought commitments for another work detail at the school on Sunday afternoon and made a list of those able to help at other sites during the week.

Pastor Hobbs said, "The Stapleford boys said if we finished cutting away the trees on the north side of the school, they would tarp the roof and get the kids back in here to finish school. The students only have a week-and-a-half before summer break. What makes my heart smile is that those kids want to be in school on Monday. That's my sweetie's doing, you know."

The rest of the team nodded and grinned at their pastor. Even the men on the crew who didn't go to his church considered him their pastor. They may not have been regular attenders at his or anybody else's church, but if anybody close to them needed marrying or burying, Calvin Hobbs was the man they wanted doing it. Pastor Hobbs called their places on the team a triple blessing. They helped finance the team, they showed up to help at the drop of a hat, and he shared the gospel with them every time they did.

An hour later, the sun had disappeared along with the last of the trees the Stapleford brothers needed removed before they tarped the roof. A few hours' work on Sunday afternoon and the building would be ready for teachers and students on Monday, as long as they avoided the north end and the gym.

Pastor Hobbs stayed around until everyone packed

their gear and departed, as was his habit. He didn't like the thought of anyone on his team forgetting anything at the site, so he double- and triple-checked each of the work areas. Someone always forgot something, this time an empty gas can and a solitary work glove. He dropped them in the back of his truck and was about to open the driver's side door when a female voice beckoned him from behind.

"Vicki? What are you still doing here?"

Vicki walked across the parking lot from the food trailer. "Same as you, I would imagine. Checking to make sure nobody left anything before I secure the trailer. Do you mind following me back to the church? Several guys are going to meet me there and load up as much as we can tonight so we can leave straight from church tomorrow."

"Sure, I can help. Hey, look, about earlier this afternoon…"

"We can talk later. I don't want to keep them waiting."

"Okay." Whatever energy Pastor Hobbs had used cutting up trees the better part of the afternoon paled in comparison to the energy his and Vicki's awkward conversation earlier had taken from him. It consumed his thoughts as he followed her back to the church. *Did I offend Vicki by not coming to the storm shelter like Janie Ruth and I always had? Doesn't she see that perceptions matter and can cause significant harm to a man in the ministry? It almost sounded like she…* He couldn't let himself go there. Could he?

29

A n hour later, Calvin and Vicki loaded the last of the canned green beans and boxes of macaroni into the trailer. Wayne would grill chicken breasts on his commercial grill to serve with vegetables, mac-n-cheese, canned fruit, and rolls. Twenty cases of water and ten cases of juice boxes were already loaded. The power company expected to restore service by Monday, so the food team would hand out their last meals at West Cary on Sunday.

With the last of the canned goods on the trailer, Pastor Hobbs went back inside to turn off the lights and lock the doors. When he returned outside ten minutes later, Shawn and Wayne were gone. Vicki had pulled the trailer from the door by the kitchen to where his S-10 was parked. He didn't see her at first, but she slid out of her truck, cutting him off from reaching his.

"Calvin, serving like this was what God designed me to do. I love helping people who can't do anything for me in return. If that's not the best representation of what Jesus did when He walked this earth, I don't know what is." She waited for a moment and when he didn't respond right away, she pressed, "Don't you think so?"

"Sure. Janie Ruth and I were on the other end of disaster after Katrina. I promised myself that once we were back on our feet, I would start a disaster relief ministry at this church. We might not be able to do every aspect, but I figured we would add an important piece to what other churches were doing. Turns out, that included chainsaws and food service. I couldn't be happier with how our church has helped people in such a significant way."

"I never want to stop. I want the Lord to use me until the day He takes me, just like Roger did. And just like Janie Ruth did."

"Me, too. But… Vicki… you seem on edge today. What's… I mean… why…?"

"Don't you see it, Calvin? Don't you?"

"No, I don't guess I…"

"That night at the dollar store. I saw you."

"Sure you did. What…"

"No, I… *saw*… you, Calvin."

"Yes, but…"

"And you noticed me, too. You leaned down and smelled your collar. And smiled."

Oh, that really was it. Before he could wrap his mind around what Vicki was revealing to him, she stepped into his personal space and looked into his eyes for confirmation. "Vicki, I…" *That scent. There it was again.*

"Tell me I'm wrong, and I won't bring it up again.

But Calvin, to put it bluntly, Janie Ruth and Roger are as dead as they're going to be. They told us to move on, all but demanded we do so. How long are we planning on waiting? I understand you loved Janie Ruth with every fiber of your being—still do. I loved Roger with every fiber of my being—still do. Don't you think...?" Her pleading brown eyes begged him to finish her sentence.

"... they would want us to put their loss behind us and move forward together?"

"Yes," she whispered, relieved.

He had imagined it. Janie Ruth's voice in his head pushed him toward Vicki the morning after he met her at the dollar store. He just couldn't move on it. If she was wrong—if *he* was wrong—the resulting fallout had the potential to destroy a friendship, a church, a ministry. But Janie Ruth wasn't wrong—*he* was. He moved the final six inches toward Vicki and kissed her softly on the mouth, just enough to cross over the line.

She stepped back and asked, "You thought about it that night, didn't you?"

"Yes."

"You asked her about us, didn't you?"

"Yes."

"What did she say?"

"She asked me what I was waiting for."

"What were you waiting for?"

"I had to be sure. I had to be okay if I was wrong."

"Me, too."

"You, too? Did you hear Roger's voice?"

"Yes, Calvin, but not how you imagine. I didn't need

him to speak after seeing you that night. In the days before he died, Roger told me if you ever showed any feelings toward me, I should snatch you up in a heartbeat."

"He said that?"

"He did. Finding somebody else was the farthest thing from my mind then and for weeks after he died. However, that night at the store, I understood what he was talking about. Today, I noticed you pulling away from me, and I didn't like it. I had to remind myself while I was serving at West Cary that you hadn't been tracking with what I had been thinking since the night at the dollar store. I'm sorry for being short with you earlier. Will you forgive me?"

"Sure. And I was tracking with you. I just tried to make myself stop."

"Well, now you don't have to." She kissed him on the cheek and climbed in her truck. Turning around before she closed the door, she added with a wink, "Sorry if you can't focus on your sermon for tomorrow."

He smiled back. "The Lord will get me through. He always does."

PASTOR HOBBS'S adrenaline pushed him into the early morning hours, trying to lock in on his text in Hebrews 6, but never making it past the first few verses. His mind kept taking him back to the dollar store, to the storm, to Vicki's shelter, to West Cary, to the kiss. Why did he feel guilty? Would the church disapprove? Had either of them grieved enough? Hadn't he always counseled people to wait at least a year after losing a spouse to make any major decisions? This qualified as one.

The voices became so crowded that concentration seemed impossible. Pastor Hobbs opened his back door and stepped out into the cool evening air. He soaked up the night sounds and took slow, deliberate breaths as his friend Easton had taught him to do in tense situations. After a few minutes, his deep breaths turned into prayers for the Lord to speak to Him.

The big clock on the living room wall, which Janie Ruth had retrieved from what remained of their house in Louisiana after Katrina, moved past two o'clock. Pastor Hobbs picked up his Bible to read through his text again. This time, the words jumped off the page at him so clearly that he shifted his eyes toward the ceiling and remarked, "That's good. They'll understand this didn't come from me."

THE NEXT MORNING Calvin arrived at the church at 6:30, an hour earlier than usual. Since the church had moved its discipleship groups into homes during the week, the church's first business on Sunday morning was their fellowship breakfast at 9:00. The men cooked for the ladies most weeks, and those in charge of the cooking this week would begin arriving about 8:00. Pastor Hobbs was there early to pray over the seats in the sanctuary before breakfast. As inspired as he was to preach the morning's message, he deemed his three hours' sleep sufficient.

Looking out his truck window at the parking spot he had used the previous night, his and Vicki's kiss seemed like a fleeting dream. He covered his boyish grin, even though no one else was around to witness it, as he entered through the side door. As he passed through row after row from the back to the front of the room, he prayed for his people's receptivity to the message he had for them today. He knew who would sit in many of those seats because they did every week, and he prayed their names to the Lord. When he reached the third row aisle seat on what would be his left side from the pulpit, he called Vicki's name and asked for clarity in their relationship. He also prayed she wouldn't distract him as he preached.

After another lap around the sanctuary to pray for the needs of his people, Pastor Hobbs finished by dropping to the altar and praying. It was his practice right before breakfast to ask the Lord to give him every word He wanted him to say to the people this morning, planned or not. After the last amen of his prayer time, he joined a jovial group of older men gathered in the fellowship hall.

As had become their custom, the cooking team counted down the final ten seconds until nine o'clock. At zero, the lead cook of the week prayed for the meal and the church service and handed Pastor Hobbs a plate. Calvin refused to go first in the beginning, but it made sense that he finish early enough to slip away for one last look at his notes before the church service began. He had eaten his scrambled eggs and was two bites into his sausage and biscuit when a friendly voice asked, "May I sit here with you, Pastor?"

He greeted her with all the outward calm he could muster. "Sure, Vicki, have a seat."

"Did you sleep well last night?"

"I stayed up until about three, working on my message. I usually spend several hours editing and revising on Saturday afternoon and run through it one more time before bed. With serving at West Cary and everything, I didn't feel like I was ready."

"And everything," she repeated with the slyest of smiles.

"Stop," he whispered, more amused than angry.

"Yes, Pastor."

"That's better. I was having a hard time focusing on the Scripture..." He had to power through a sneaky smile to finish. "... so I stepped outside to soak in God's presence. It worked because when I came back in, I read a part of today's passage that didn't jump out to me on Monday morning when I first read it. It came alive at two o'clock this morning, though. Check this out." He pulled an index card from his pocket, which she read aloud:

Hebrews 6:10-12: God is not unjust; he will not forget your work and the love you have shown him as you have helped his people and continue to help them. We want each of you to show this same diligence to the very end, so that what you hope for may be fully realized. We do not want you to become lazy, but to imitate those who through faith and patience inherit what has been promised.

"Oh, Calvin, I have so much running through my mind right now."

"Right?"

Maudie Simpkins sat her plate on the table beside Vicki's and wiggled her ample body into the chair next to her. "Am I interrupting anything?"

Vicki never skipped a beat. "No, Maudie, we were just talking about the Scripture Calvin is preaching from this morning. How in the world are you?"

"Oh, fair to middlin'. Bursitis's been actin' up a bit but haven't had a migraine in better'n a week, so you take what you can get at our age, right?"

Pastor Hobbs almost choked on a piece of bacon. Maudie hadn't seen Vicki's age in at least ten years. "Maudie, I'm glad you're doing well. Did the storm do any damage to your garden?"

"Not to speak of. That late frost got me earlier this year, though. Had to replant all my t'maters."

"What a shame. I'm glad the storm didn't destroy your garden. I know you enjoy working it."

"Got room for one more?" Cordelia Blyson pulled out the chair next to Maudie and joined her and Vicki and Calvin. She was about Maudie's age and in charge of the church newsletter. She never missed an opportunity to put someone on the prayer list.

"Cordelia, I was just about to tell Calvin that we've

been trying to get Vicki to join our women's Bible study group."

"Maudie, I've already told you I'm in a group." Vicki's response was direct but politely short of snippy. "I'm content with my group."

"You've said that, but perhaps you'll reconsider, with your recent life change and all."

"She's right," Cordelia said. "We widows have to stick together. Plus," she added, leaning toward Vicki and whispering, "the deacons are good about taking care of us as long as we let them know what our needs are."

"Oh, I get it," Vicki said. Calvin could tell that she was enjoying the response circulating in her mind. "So if, say, I've got a tree down on my place, I would call the deacons, and they would come cut it up for me?"

"Dear, you wouldn't have to bother them. You just call me and consider it done."

"Even if I can afford to pay a tree company to come cut it up and remove it for me?"

Cordelia sat back, satisfied. "Like I said, being in our little widows' group has its advantages."

"And I should take advantage of them?"

"Why wouldn't you? You've earned it."

Vicki swallowed the curt response on the tip of her tongue. Instead, her smile dripped sweetness. "Well, I certainly will consider the widows' group."

"Oh, that's wonderful," said Maudie. "We would be so glad to have you. Pastor, don't you think that's wonderful?"

Calvin dodged. "I hadn't considered Vicki's

attending the widows' group. I guess it's up to her, but I'm sure she appreciates your hospitality. Ladies, it's been a pleasure, but I need to give my message a last once-over, so if you'll excuse me?" As he stood to leave, he sneaked a wink to Vicki.

30

"As I consider the implications of Hebrews 6:10-12, I believe it is important that we focus on the work we have done for God in the past, not for His favor but because we love Him. I don't remember ever talking to a Christian who didn't feel closer to God when he or she was serving others. Verse ten tells us that serving others equates to loving God. So many of you spent your Saturday with me at West Cary High School, cutting trees away from the school and serving food to those affected by yesterday's tornado. I suspect there are some tired and sore bodies among you today. Still, I dare say none of you would trade what you experienced yesterday for a ball game on TV or a nap in your recliner or a day of shopping or whatever you would have otherwise done with your day.

"For those of us who may have entered new stages of life—whether job situation or parenting stage or loss of a spouse—I believe verse eleven is an encouragement from the Lord that our work is not finished. This verse stood out to me as I read through this message again in the peaceful night air on my back deck in the wee hours of this morning. My Janie Ruth realized her hope a few months ago, but I have never known anyone so diligent to the very end. My moment of peace was not in celebrating her, though we have all done plenty of that together. No, the Lord's still small voice this morning challenged me to stay diligent to the very end, too. The end of my wife's time here on earth was not the end of mine. Oh, I wanted my time to coincide with hers, but the Lord has more work for me. Over the past few months, I have had times where I've felt sorry for myself and wondered why He didn't take me, too. Serving other people in the name of the Lord pushes me out of my self-centeredness. It doesn't totally get my mind off my problems like you might imagine, but serving others helps me see them from God's perspective.

"Verse twelve warns us of the consequences of spending too much time focused inward. Nobody sets out to be lazy or sluggish, but it happens. How? For me, I look back and realize the more time I spent focused on myself or my loss was less time spent doing the work the Lord had left for me to do. My work is to serve my church and to do my best to reach lost people with the gospel. A lazy Christian is an ineffective Christian, and that's not what I wanted to become. God has taught me that laziness is not one big decision, but tens and hundreds of tiny decisions to do nothing. Don't get me wrong—it's difficult to push aside the resistance. I have counseled people for whom it would be a major win to get out of bed in the morning; if that's you, win that battle to get to your feet. Win that one and move on to the next one. Win that one and the next one after that and the one after that until you've built momentum. Eventually, the obstacles that seemed so insurmountable turn into habits of perseverance. These are habits of faith that the One we do not see is working in us in our individual strings of victories over spiritual laziness to continue building the kingdom He wants to build through us.

"My body will scream for a nap this afternoon, but I will go to West Cary with a chainsaw instead. The Lord will give me sleep in His time. For now, I can serve Him best by showing up over there today to show that community that God sees them in their troubles and provides for them in their difficulties. One or more of them may connect what we are doing for them physically to what God wants to do for them spiritually. That may happen today or it might happen later, and I may recognize when it makes an eternal impact and I may not, but that's up to God to decide. It's my job to keep showing up to serve others, even when my physical body would rather take a break. You let the Holy Spirit tell you what these verses mean for you."

Pastor Hobbs closed the message with an invitation for his people to respond. The choir sang through the final chorus twice before everyone finished doing business with the Lord at the altars. He would have loved to linger longer than usual and hear how God had spoken to his people. Instead, he hurried out the door to change into his work clothes and join his chainsaw team at West Cary. Their response to his message would give him a sense of how it came across.

"HEY, PASTOR." John "Early" Higgins greeted Calvin as he joined his team to cut up two of the trees they had felled on Saturday but not had time to finish. "We're ready, but we waited to eat until you got here. While we've been waiting, we came up with an idea for you."

"Yeah, what's that, Early?"

"We've decided you should leave your Saturday sermon prep to the wee hours of the morning every week. I believe that was the finest sermon we've heard you preach."

"Thanks, Early. That means a lot coming from you guys who are already living out Hebrews six. I'm not so sure I'm on board with three hours of sleep before church on Sunday, though."

"Oh, I'm just kidding, but none of us are joking about the message today. Let's go eat and get some caffeine in you so you don't nod off on us while holding a saw."

"Sounds good. Let's eat."

Many of the residents who lived near West Cary had come and gone already. They had assembled their own chainsaw crews to work on the most pressing areas at one another's homes. The workers from the power company repairing the downed power lines would eat in shifts, but the feeding area was sparse when Calvin's crew lined up. They moved through the line and followed others around the corner for a chicken breast from Wayne Simpkins' grill. After Maudie's brother-in-law plopped a piece of barbecued bird on his plate, Calvin took a seat at one of the empty tables to wait on his crew. Before the next man came around the corner, Vicki walked over balancing six bottles of water between her hands.

"Wonderful message, Pastor," she said.

"Thank you, Ms. Stapleford." He held her gaze until the next man sat down beside him.

"Get this man some caffeine, Vicki," Early Higgins said, sliding into the seat on the other side of his pastor. "He might preach better with three hours' sleep, but I don't trust him as much running a chainsaw all sleep deprived."

"You got it. I was just telling him what a wonderful message it was. Coffee or soda, Pastor?"

"Coffee, please."

"Coming up."

A few minutes later, Vicki placed a cup of steaming brew on the table. Calvin noticed Early Higgins glance up at her and then at him. His mouth dropped open ever so slightly, but he swallowed whatever idea he had. For his part, Calvin thanked Vicki with only a half glance up at her.

FOUR HOURS LATER, the chainsaw crew finished their work and loaded the trucks and trailers. Pastor Hobbs dismissed his crew with his thanks for living out his message from church throughout the afternoon. "Sleep well tonight, my brothers. Great job this weekend. I'm going to take my last walk around, so I'll see you guys during the week."

The only stray item was a long-sleeve T-shirt Jeff Dankins had left sitting on a stump after the afternoon temperatures and the intensity of the work rose. When Calvin reached down to get it, he caught a flicker of light out of the corner of his eye when the lights in the school office powered back to life. He texted his men to inform them the power had been restored and walked toward his truck with a smile plastered wide across his worn face.

"What are you so happy about, mister?" Vicki asked from the food trailer she was locking when he approached.

"Power's back on."

"I saw that."

"Perfect way to end the day, right?"

"Perhaps, but I had another idea."

Calvin tilted his head. "What's that?"

"I know you're tired and probably ready to go home, get cleaned up, and go to bed."

"But?"

"But everything that needs cleaning up on this trailer

can wait until tomorrow, and the sunsets are so pretty from my back deck."

"I don't know, Vicki."

"Oh, come on, it'll be fine."

"What if people talk?"

"Park your truck out back where no one can see it. If anybody says anything, we'll say we were parking the food trailer, which we will do so you're not lying. Don't you suspect we need to get out in front of this... whatever we decide to call it?"

"That's for sure. Early Higgins almost said something when you set the coffee on the table for me earlier."

"I overheard Shonda Maples go 'mm hmm' under her breath when I started walking back to your table with the coffee. Come on, let's get going."

"Vicki, I..."

"I make a mean sweet tea."

"See you there."

———

"So we watched the sunset and sipped sweet tea and decided to call our 'whatever we decide to call it' a courtship. I met with my deacons the next night after Vicki and I had both told our kids earlier in the day. I trusted our deacons to help me steer folks in the right direction. You understand how people talk, especially since Janie Ruth and I were such close friends with Vicki and Roger for so many years before our spouses passed.

You just never know what dots they might incorrectly connect."

Easton said, "I'm curious about the meeting with the deacons. How did that go?"

Calvin laughed. "Well, seeing as Early Higgins and Fred Maples—that's Shonda Maples' husband—are two of my three deacons, Sonny Sanford was the only one caught by surprise. They considered it as natural as breathing that God would draw Vicki and me to each other, and they also figured it might be best if the church learned about it from me. I told them it would be a test of who could stay quiet for two days before our Wednesday night supper. They promised word would not leak through them, so I felt confident we could tell the church before anyone found out."

PASTOR HOBBS SAT down with his Wednesday night meal of chicken strips, green beans, mashed potatoes and gravy, a roll, and a healthy portion of Betty Lou Waller's death by chocolate concoction. The church didn't have a full-blown service on Wednesday nights, but they enjoyed a meal together in the fellowship hall and prayed for one another. In between supper and the prayer time, Calvin would share a short devotional. He would use that time this week to reflect on his Sunday message and reveal his and Vicki's courtship.

"May I sit here with you, Pastor?"

"Sure, have a seat." Calvin pulled the chair next to him

out for Maudie Simpkins. "Here, let me set your tea down for you." Before Maudie was settled, Cordelia Blyson took the seat on the other side of Calvin. She started straight in on what wonderful reports she was getting from all the people who served with the disaster relief team. Next week's newsletter was going to be an easy one to write, she said, especially in light of Calvin's message on Sunday.

"Y'all have room for one more?" Vicki asked, sitting her plate and drink on the other side of Maudie. "Hey, look, it's our Sunday morning crew. Good evening, everybody."

Maudie's quick greeting transitioned into another invitation for Vicki to enlist in the widows' discipleship group. "We meet on Friday at noon, like we have for years. You ought to join us this week."

"Maudie, you understand I still work some at our construction company, right?"

"Aw, honey, you own the company, don't you? Your boys can handle it for a few hours, can't they?"

"Tell you what—I'll think on it."

"You've been saying that long enough," Cordelia blurted. "Calvin, you tell Vicki to set her pride aside and come join us this week. You know we always have plenty to eat, and she looks like she could use a little fattening up." Calvin and Vicki both choked back laughs, and Vicki excused herself to get a napkin.

Maudie and Cordelia used the opportunity to pelt Calvin with reasons for Vicki's coming to their widows' group. Vicki lingered at the table up front, greeting the deacons while focusing on the table she had just left. They saw Calvin lift both of his index fingers and invite the ladies closer to share a secret with them. They didn't hear him ask them not to take offense, but Vicki was moving in a different direction than their group. When Pastor Hobbs excused himself, walked to the front of the room, and made the announcement, they heard Maudie cackling above the cheers throughout the room. She shouted, "Cordelia, oh, Cordelia, you've been scooped!" Laughter filled the fellowship hall as Cordelia turned every shade of red.

"Vicki and I have been courting for a few months with the blessing and encouragement of our church. Since this group meant so much to me last year when I was at my lowest point, I thought it appropriate to announce here that we will be married on New Year's Eve."

The room erupted with applause. Vicki joined Calvin at the front and slipped her arm around his waist.

Pastor Hobbs motioned for quiet and continued, "We wanted the wedding to be a small one, but we couldn't *not* invite anyone from our church. We want to invite each of you to come, even those of you we haven't met until today. You are so special to me and, by extension, Vicki, so our invitation is not just a polite one. We genuinely want you to be a part of our celebration."

Vicki pointed toward the back at the Turner tables. "Carol, you love engagement and baby announcements, so you've got to be on cloud nine here tonight."

Carol was beaming. "You better know I am. I am so

proud of you two. Congratulations from all the Turners! Now, let's take a gander at the ring I suspect you have."

Vicki pulled the ring from her purse and slipped it on her finger. A crowd gathered around her as everyone added their well wishes.

In the front corner of the room, Austen Thomason leaned over to Laticia Brooks and said, "Looks like everybody's getting married except me."

AUSTEN

31

"Girl, don't go there," Laticia pleaded.

"I know," Austen said. "It just seems everybody here is getting married but me."

"Yeah, but don't let that pressure get to you. You need to remember the original Lonesome, Party of Six folks all came in here figuring they were the loneliest people in the world. They're all doing just fine—better than okay—in a year's time. That's because of you."

"You're right. I apologize for the pity party."

"I understand you. But don't let the enemy take what you meant for good and turn it around on you. He's crafty, you know."

"Just a fleeting notion, that's all. I am happier than I imagined at this point last year. One random thing has led to so much more than I dreamed."

"Girl, you'll never convince me it was random." Laticia leaned in closer. "You got your hopes up when Easton came in here earlier tonight. You've got to admit he looks good with Sherrill, though. Want me to ask if she has a brother?"

"No, don't ask. When the Lord is ready to send me a husband, I want to be sure he came from the Lord and not from my meddling."

"I hear you."

"And not everybody's got engagements or new boyfriends or new grandkids to celebrate, so there's plenty of hope left for me."

"Like Pops."

"Pops?"

"Mr. Jimmy Lee's not engaged." Both girls burst out laughing. Everyone else remained gathered around Calvin and Vicki, offering their congratulations. "But, hey, maybe he has like a great-great nephew you would like."

"Stop!"

"I'm just messing with you. Where do you reckon the group goes from here? I mean, this was a natural reunion, but I'm not sure where we'd meet a year from now if it keeps growing like this."

"There will be plenty of time to talk about it throughout the year if we show up to all this year's weddings."

"Girl, you got that right. I hate I won't be here to go to 'em with you."

"Could be we'll celebrate a mini-reunion in Charlotte next year?"

"Oh, no, girl, if we get married, it will be right here in Harriston, where Robert's folks live, and we will invite y'all, for sure. You can bring your Mr. Right if you've met him by then."

"Keep dreaming." Austen's countenance turned serious. "Laticia, I'm glad we've gotten to be close friends over this last year. I love your relentless optimism. I realize you didn't choose the circumstances of your childhood, but they shaped you into a resilient person who always sees hope for everyone. Trust me, I needed that."

"Thanks, and right back at you. You try to put yourself in other people's shoes and figure out a way to encourage them." Laticia reached for a hug. "Austen, when we stayed up all night last year talking about our Lonesome, Party of Six, it was like we had been sisters our whole lives. Girl, you're my best friend. I could tell you anything and trust you would speak truth to me."

"Same here." Austen's eyes scanned the room, finding last year's six. "Hey, do you remember what we called all of them when we stayed up all night talking about them?"

"Sure do." Laticia pointed to them as she called them out. "Pops, One Month Sober, Mr. Important, Pastor Widower, Army Mom, and Inconvenient Heart Attack."

"Now that we're part of their lives, we should invent new nicknames for them."

"I'm down with that. What amazes me about this whole crew—they all appeared so isolated when all they needed was someone to listen. It didn't even need to be a family member or close friend, just someone who cared enough to let them talk. Where do you want to start?"

"Let's begin with Pops. What a sweet old man. Without a doubt, he's the youngest-acting ninety-three-year-old I've ever met. Everybody in this room adores him."

"Shoot, everybody in this town adores him. All he wanted was somebody to call him by name."

"Mr. Jimmy Lee. Something so simple as saying the man's name reconnected him to the world."

"If all he wanted was somebody to call his name, let's do him the honor."

"I agree. *Mr. Jimmy Lee* will do just fine for him. Or *Mr. Flirt*, if he wants a different nickname. Or *The Big Fish*."

"Ooh, girl, I like that one. Let's go with that one —*Mr. Jimmy Lee, the Big Fish*."

"Done." Austen opened her notes app to record their work. "Who's next?"

"One Month Sober—Tara Cates. Talk about right place, right time... no telling what would have happened to that girl if she had walked outta here when she finished eating last Thanksgiving. Austen, you saved that girl's life by what you did. You can't tell it by looking at her tonight, but she was downright fragile last year."

"We could be friends. Her little boy is adorable, too. She showed me some pictures of him on her phone. I'm going to see is she wants to hang out some, especially after you're gone—sniff, sniff. For real, though, she needs another nickname. Any ideas?"

"Well, she's made a lot of progress this year. Her year has been all about forgiveness—giving it and receiving it and piling up the chips and coins for her progress. Something about that, maybe?"

"How about instead of One Month Sober, we call her *Thirteen Months Clean* this year?"

"I like that, too, Austen. That would encourage her."

"Okay, who's next?"

"Mr. Important—Easton Sterling. Have you forgiven him for breaking your heart?"

"Stop messing with me. I don't give my heart away that easily."

Laticia elbowed Austen and whispered, "Yeah, but you gave your eyes away when he walked in tonight. Don't deny it."

"I can neither confirm nor deny. I'm happy for him and Sherrill."

"Yeah, he's smitten with her. I was wondering if he had it in him. He's got a new old career, a new girlfriend. He's made plenty of changes."

"How about *Mr. Perspective*? No, we can do better than that. Wait, what if we call him *New Scoreboard*?"

"Ooh, I like that. Fits him…"

"Like a glove?"

"Austen, girl, you've got it going on. Who's next?"

"Pastor Widower. I still can't bring myself to call him Calvin."

"Me, neither. I have so much respect for him. I know he ain't perfect—nobody is—but he sure is a respectable man. He's fixing to marry a second fine wife, too."

"God has been kind to Pastor Hobbs, for sure."

"And *through* him. This could be a tough one. Let's see—what stands out to you from his story?"

"That his work's not finished yet."

"Yeah, you're right, although *Pastor Work's Not Done Yet* seems too long."

"How about *Pastor Future* or something similar?"

"Hey, you know how preachers like to start all their points with the same letter?"

"Alliteration."

"Yeah, I might have slept through that in English class. Like you say, I can neither confirm nor deny. But how about *Pastor Promise*?"

"Done." Austen typed it into her phone. "Next?"

"Army Mom."

"Paula—I just love her. She sure has led an interesting life."

"Interesting—I guess that's one way to put it. I'll take boring any day over what that woman's gone through, but the Lord has given her back the years the locusts have eaten away, as my pastor says."

"My pastor says that, too. It's from the book of Joel or one of the other minor prophets. I get them all confused."

"Wherever it is, Paula is a walking, talking example of it. Austen, you should have seen that woman last year. She'd have just as soon spit at you than talk to you. You could tell when their little group started talking, she realized hers wasn't the only sob story in the house. By the time they finished, she had stopped feeling sorry for herself. She walked outta here with her head held high like she was ready to take on the world."

"And, boy, has she. She's amazing."

"Let me try this one. She's been so much about her

kids, she hadn't thought about herself much. And who else do you know who would forgive somebody that walked out on her so long ago and give him another chance to be in her kids' lives? How about we call her *Second Chance*, like the one she's receiving from God and the one she's offering?"

"Awesome—got it. Next?"

"Inconvenient Heart Attack. She sure needs a new nickname."

"Carol Turner. Another incredible woman. How lucky is it for her kids to have her as a mom, huh?"

"Girl, you nailed it. I'm sure she's got her issues, but she's as solid as they come. I'm going to tell you, though, she looked anything but solid last year. She grew up real sheltered, and she looked like she had slipped back into her shell for the longest time when they were all sitting here talking. She loosened up when she saw she wasn't the only one going through a lonely time. Goes to show, no matter people's station in life, we all share the same basic emotions."

"For sure."

Laticia sat up straight with a bolt of inspiration. "Hey, I got Ms. Carol. She'll add two sons-in-law and a grandbaby to her family, right? More grandkids sure to follow. But she's also gonna have a lot more kids real soon."

"What do you mean?"

"You said her kids were lucky to have her as their mom?"

"Yeah."

"Well, how do you imagine folks our age will feel

when they read her book? They're gonna wish their mama was like her."

"Right, so…"

Laticia drew up to a proud pose. "Ms. Carol is *Everybody's Mama.*"

"I love it! Okay, that's all. Should we tell them?"

"Why not? They'd get a kick out of our nicknames for them—old and new."

"Think you can get everybody's attention to tell them before folks start leaving?"

"Austen, first of all, nobody is leaving here tonight without saying goodbye to you. And second, can I get people's attention? Watch and learn."

32

Laticia stuck her pinkies inside the corners of her mouth and let out a whistle so shrill Austen covered her ears. The room came to a standstill, and Laticia announced in a normal tone, "Austen has one last presentation she would like to make before anybody slips out of here tonight."

Austen stepped forward, poised and confident. "Thanks, Laticia. Now, to take you back a few hours less than 365 days ago, Laticia was introducing all of you to me at my apartment. It took all night long because she didn't want to miss a single detail, and neither did I. She had to start off by describing you since I wouldn't have known you by your names then. We thought it might be a super cool way to wrap up tonight by telling you those original nicknames, along with some new ones we made up for you. Sound good?"

Lonesome, Party of Six and their guests liked the

idea. Austen waited for the well-wishers to meander to their seats and turn their attention toward her.

"Okay," Austen began, "we're going to read your last year's name and this year's name. Mr. Jimmy Lee, we called you *Pops* last year like most people do, but we want to honor you by calling you by your name to show how much we value you for being you. But... in case that's not enough for you, we'll call you *Mr. Jimmy Lee Yates, the Big Fish.*" Austen continued down her list, calling each of the original group by name and having that person stand. She shared each person's previous year's name, summarized the growth she and Laticia had noticed through their stories, and gave them their new monikers. Each of the original six was pleased and honored by the gesture.

When Austen completed her list, she stepped toward her seat, but Easton stopped her. "No, ma'am, Austen, you're not finished yet. You either, Laticia. Get up there and join your partner in crime. I have some names for you two.

"Laticia, let's start with you. Last year, we may have known you as *Hostess*. You're the one who knew who had paid for our meals and stuck with us to make sure we ate way more pie and drank way more coffee than we needed. If not for you, Austen's good deed would have remained just that, nothing more. Your part was to connect us to one another that night and with Austen later. You excel at caring for people and connecting them to others. That will serve you well at the corporate level as you move on to bigger things. For your part in our story, how about we call you *Catalyst*?"

"Thank you," Laticia answered, humbled by the gesture. "I like that just fine, and I'll remember it when I start my new position."

"Our party of six got together before tonight—virtually, that is—and chose a gift for you, Laticia." He pulled a bag from under the table and reached into it to produce a beautiful brushed nickel desk lamp. "When we decided on this, we didn't realize you had a new job, but we knew you would graduate soon and do something incredible with your life. You are a bright light in this world, and we want you to remember there is a group of people who have seen you at your best and who believe in you. This lamp has a three-way bulb. You're the second light, Laticia. If you twist the switch a little, the bulb will come on, but it's dim. Keep twisting and you'll get to the brightest light, but not until you go through the catalyst, the second one. You remember us when you click through that second light to make your room brighter. We love you, girl."

Laticia was crying as she grinned, like a burst of rain on a sunny day. She accepted the lamp from Easton and read the plate screwed to its base: *To our very special hostess. Love, Lonesome, Party of Six*. "Thank you, Easton. Thank you all. I can't tell y'all how much this means to me. I will treasure it."

"Austen, your turn," Easton said. "Even though we've said it every way we can imagine, our words cannot accurately express our thanks to you. Throughout the past twelve months, we've known you as *Mystery Benefactor* or *Laticia's Friend*. We did our best to find of a gift worthy of our appreciation, and it connects well to the name we've chosen for you. I have here six different restaurant gift cards, one from each of us. They are worth two hundred dollars each, and they are for you to give away as you see fit. Don't stop with us, Austen. The outcome might not be the same as ours, but we hope you'll keep noticing lonely people and reaching out to them. And just to make sure you don't forget your original Lonesome, Party of Six..."

Easton reached back into his bag and pulled out a thick cloth. He handed Sherrill a corner and opened a gorgeous handmade quilt. A variety of Log Cabin T-shirts comprised the quilt's inner sections. "We hope this will remind you of the comfort you once gave six lonely souls when you covered our meal here at The Log Cabin. Because you cared enough to reach out to us in our time of loneliness, we dub you *Miss Altruism*."

Austin bounced up and down, her hands clasped in front of her chin. "Miss Altruism. I love it! Oh, I can't even tell you how much I love it! When I was in high school, my English teacher would read our vocabulary list and have us pick out the word we liked best. He called it our five-dollar word of the week. One time, the first word was *altruism*, and I was drawn to it like a magnet. I memorized it for the quiz that week and haven't forgotten it. *Altruism: the principle or practice of unselfish concern for or devotion to the welfare of others.* For you guys to see that in me is beyond special. Thank you."

An hour later, no one had left. When the grandfather clock in the corner of the room struck ten—albeit at 10:07—the Turner family bid everyone goodnight, emptying almost half the room. Others followed until only Tara, Austen, and Laticia remained.

Tara asked, "Austen, would you be interested in coming over to my house for a movie tomorrow night? It's Zan's night to stay at my mom and dad's, so our choices won't be limited to animated movies."

"I would love to, thanks. What movies do you like?"

"Anything non-animated on Friday nights."

"Oh, animated movies aren't so bad. I enjoyed them with my brother after most kids my age had stopped watching them."

"Me, too."

"But I understand. Let's pick a chick flick, shall we?"

"Yes, yes we shall." Tara and Austen swapped phone numbers, and Tara gave her the address before departing for the evening.

Laticia wrapped her arms around Austen. "You did good tonight. I'm so proud of you, and I'm gonna miss you like nobody's business. I'm glad you got a new friend to hang out with after I move."

"You're the best, Laticia. It has been quite a journey together."

Laticia stepped back to lock eyes with Austen, her hands still grasping her friend's shoulders. "Don't stop, girl. Never stop be being you. It's people like you who change the world."

LONESOME, PARTY OF SIX SERIES

Lonesome, Party of Six

Lonesome Reunion

Two of a Kind: Working on an Empty House

Twenty Years Gone: Lonesome in the Heart of Texas

Broken Pane

Everybody Else's Wedding

www.ingramcontent.com/pod-product-compliance
Lightning Source LLC
Chambersburg PA
CBHW020411260626
47156CB00007B/2329